BRITTANY BUTTERFIELD

If Brittany had been paying attention to what was going on around her, she might have noticed that she was being followed when she left the party. But the cool air outside felt so good, it didn't occur to her to be afraid.

Not until she had walked about a block and heard the footsteps behind her.

Startled, she spun around just in time to see someone diving into the bushes along the sidewalk a few yards back.

Joey Kulaga. She should have known it was him.

Her heart started pounding wildly. She turned and started walking again, more quickly this time, looking straight ahead.

As she rounded the corner, a dark figure jumped out in front of her and grabbed her arm.

Brittany opened her mouth to scream, but nothing came out.

"Shhh . . . it's me," someone whispered.

"Nathan?" She stared up at him. "What are you doing here?"

"What are *you* doing here, all by yourself, at night? Joey Kulaga is following you."

"You *know* who he is?" she asked in disbelief.

"Yeah, I know who he is," Nathan said in a tone that told Brittany exactly what he thought of Joey. "Shhh . . . he's coming. Stay there. I mean it, Brittany, don't move."

She nodded numbly. Then Nathan slipped around the corner.

A few seconds later, she heard a bone-chilling scream, and it hadn't come from Nathan.

WENDY CORSI STAUB

BRITTANY BUTTERFIELD
AND THE
BACK-TO-SCHOOL BLUES

Z·FAVE
KENSINGTON PUBLISHING CORP.

Z*FAVE BOOKS are published by

Kensington Publishing Corp.
850 Third Avenue
New York, NY 10022

Z*FAVE and the Z*FAVE logo Reg. U.S. Pat. & TM Off.

First Printing: August, 1995

Printed in the United States of America

*For Uncle Lorrie, Aunt Marian, Jill, and JoLynne Corsi
and for my husband, Mark, with love*

*And in memory of another special angel,
Frances Ginsberg*

Prologue

Nathan Oakley was lounging on the grass in the Holding Garden, reading *Yankee Magazine* and eating a Baby Ruth candy bar. He wasn't in heaven—not yet, anyway—but this was the next best place.

Who would have dreamed that being dead would be like this? Oh, sure, Nathan missed his parents and sister and the house where he had grown up in the small midwestern town of Silver Falls. But there weren't many other things he'd missed ever since the June day in 1983 when, during a senior class outing at Adventureland, the Whirling Twirl-a-Curl ride had malfunctioned, sending Nathan and three of his friends hurtling through the air.

He'd never given life after death much thought before then, but when he had considered it, he'd vaguely imagined drifting white clouds and pearly gates.

He had seen huge, gleaming gates when he'd first arrived, but they'd looked like they were made of gold, not pearl. And once he'd passed through the gates, nothing was as he'd imagined.

First of all, there was Celeste, the golden-haired beauty dressed in a khaki uniform and wearing a name badge that said "Guide." She'd greeted Nathan with such a warm hug that his last lingering attachment to his mortal life had disappeared in a *poof.*

The first thing he'd seen when he looked around were the three friends who had accompanied him on the Whirling Twirl-a-Curl: Maddie Parpelli, his next-door neighbor; Thea Caruthers, Maddie's best friend; and Bryan O'Brock, Thea's boyfriend. They had all looked like Nathan felt: a little dazed, but oddly contented at the same time.

And no wonder. They were in the most incredible place Nathan had ever seen. It was a lush paradise of flowers and chirping birds, sun-dappled groves and waterfalls, and meadows with grass as cushy as plush carpeting.

Celeste had said that this was called the Holding Garden. "It's kind of like a big waiting area—a place where new arrivals are sent," she'd explained during orientation.

At first, Nathan had interpreted that to mean that this was sort of like a rest area on the way to heaven. But he'd soon found out that it wasn't quite that simple.

"You're all here for a reason," Celeste had announced. "Your preliminary earthbound assignments were cut short. As a result, you need to complete the program by alternate means."

Nathan and his friends had eventually figured out what *that* meant. They all had unfinished business to resolve before they'd be allowed to move on to their final reward: heaven.

Maddie had already received her assignment. She hadn't been around much lately, and she wasn't allowed to talk about what she was up to.

Meanwhile, Nathan, Thea, and Bryan had hung out here in the Holding Garden. Nathan had no idea how much time had passed since they'd arrived. It might have been days, or months, or even years—somehow, it was impossible to keep track around here, and it didn't seem to matter.

Meanwhile, new arrivals drifted through the gates all the time. Nathan couldn't help noticing that they were all pretty young—teenagers, or adults who couldn't be older than their twenties and thirties. Every race seemed to be represented, and there were people from all over the world, mingling like old friends.

Nathan had always been the shy type, but here it was impossible not to make new friends. He'd had some great conversations about the Yankees with Sal and Joey, construction workers from the Bronx who had shown up after their scaffolding collapsed. He'd gotten involved in some good-natured arguments with Robbie and Kate, Met fans who arrived with a crowd of other passengers from a plane that had crashed.

And then there was Julia, who had come through the gates alone while Nathan was hanging around talking to Thea one day. Julia had been ill for a long time back on earth, Nathan later found out, but here her skin glowed and her eyes twinkled and she was lighthearted again at last. Nathan couldn't help being drawn to Julia, and Thea and Bryan were always teasing him about having a crush on her.

Now, as Nathan flipped a page of his *Yankee Magazine* and popped the last of his Baby Ruth candy bar into his mouth, he heard Julia calling him.

"Nathan! Look," she said, coming through a grove of blooming lilac bushes, with Thea and Bryan on her heels.

"What's that?" he asked, staring at the folded sheet of paper she was waving at him.

"Celeste said to give it to you." Thea pushed her long hair behind her ears, and Nathan noticed that she was wearing yet another different pair of earrings.

"You know what that note means, buddy," Bryan added, around the ever-present toothpick he was chewing on.

Nathan nodded. He knew what Bryan meant. Maddie had received a written summons from Celeste when it was time to start her assignment.

Julia handed the paper over, and Nathan unfolded it carefully.

He read it over silently, then looked up at his three curious friends and nodded. "This is it, all right. It's time."

"For your assignment?" Thea asked.

"Yup." He refolded the paper, tucked it into the back pocket of his jeans, and exhaled.

"Are you nervous?" Julia asked, touching his sleeve.

"Not nervous, exactly," he said, trying to figure out what it was that he was feeling. "More like . . ."

"Excited?" Bryan supplied.

"Yeah, I guess that must be it." Nathan tucked his *Yankee Magazine* under his arm and looked around at the three of them. "Um, I've got to get going. See you guys."

"Sure—we'll see you soon," Thea said, reaching out and hugging him. "I mean, Maddie's always popping in and out of here, even though she's on assignment."

"Yeah, that's right," Bryan said, clapping Nathan on the back.

But they all knew it wasn't going to be the same. Once Maddie had gotten her summons, it was like she was separated from the rest of them—like she was part of some secret society.

Now it was Nathan's turn.

He looked at Julia.

She smiled. "Good luck," she said in her lighthearted way, but her eyes looked a little wistful.

"Thanks," Nathan said. He reached out and gave her a quick hug.

Then he adjusted his navy and white baseball cap and headed off to meet Celeste.

He found her by the gates, and she grinned when she saw him. "Nathan," she said warmly. "Are you ready?"

"Yup," he said, trying to sound confident. "All set."

"Good. Now, you remember what I went over with you in orientation, don't you? About getting an assignment?"

He nodded. "It's something I have to do before I earn my wings and get to go to heaven."

"Exactly. Do you have any questions?"

"Only about a million of them." He cleared

his throat. "Like, will the wings just sprout on my back, or what?"

Celeste laughed. "They're not actual wings, Nathan. It's just an expression."

"Oh," he said, feeling foolish.

"What other questions do you have?"

"Uh, that's it, for now, I guess," he said, not wanting to risk looking like an idiot again.

"Okay, then, all you have to do is come with me, and I'll introduce you to Angela. She'll explain the rest."

"Who's Angela?"

"You'll see," Celeste said with a mysterious smile. "Come on."

She took his hand and led him toward the gates.

He hadn't been on the other side since he'd arrived, and hadn't been able to remember much of what he'd seen in those fleeting moments. All he really recalled was a blinding light that beckoned him toward the gates.

Now, as he followed Celeste through them again, he discovered that everything was misty and hushed beyond the Holding Garden—sort of like what he'd always imagined heaven to look like. Only this wasn't heaven.

For an instant he could have sworn he heard far-off tinkling music, but then it faded.

"Angela?" Celeste called, looking around.

Instantly, she appeared—a pretty young

woman with big black eyes and wavy black hair tumbling past her shoulders. She wore flat creamy leather boots and vanilla-colored leggings under a big, soft ivory cable-knit sweater.

"Hi!" Angela said brightly, grinning at Nathan.

"Hi," he said, staring. He didn't think he'd ever seen her before, but there was something oddly familiar about her . . .

"I'm Angela. And you're Nathan," she added.

"Right." He nodded, though it hadn't been a question. She clearly knew who he was, and she was looking at him almost . . . fondly?

"Nathan, Angela has been your guardian angel," Celeste announced.

"She has? You have?" he said, turning from Celeste back to Angela.

"Yup," she said proudly.

"Have we ever met?"

Angela and Celeste exchanged a glance, and Nathan thought he saw Celeste nod slightly, as if giving Angela permission to reveal something.

"Not that you'd remember," Angela told him. "It's just easier that way."

"What do you mean? Easier what way?"

"During our preliminary earthbound assignment—human life, to be more specific—our memories of encounters with our guardian angels simply . . . fade," Angela said.

"Oh." Nathan pondered this for a moment. "So what you're telling me is that you've been around me, but I've just forgotten all about it."

"Right," Angela and Celeste said in unison.

"But you seem kind of familiar," he said, shaking his head and looking intently at her.

"Well, I'm sure there are traces of me left in your mind," she said, smiling. "I'm not *that* easy to forget."

"Yeah, but I can't seem to grasp the memories," he said, squeezing his eyes closed and concentrating. "It's like they're on the fringes of my mind . . ."

"I was there that day in 1975 when you and Daryl Mearns decided to wait out that thunderstorm under a tree," Angela prodded helpfully.

Nathan's eyes snapped open. "You know about that?"

"Of course. I know about *everything*," she said simply. "How do you think you avoided getting struck by lightning that day?"

"You're kidding. You saved us?"

"I saved *you*." Angela shrugged as if it were no big deal, but Nathan could see a hint of pride in her eyes. "Daryl's angel saved him."

"Wow."

"There were other times, too," she said, sounding a little like she were bragging.

"Really? When?"

"Angela?" Celeste cut in pointedly, before she could say anything else. "I don't think there's time for this now."

"You're right. Come on, Nathan. We'd better move it." Angela took his arm and started leading him away.

Startled, he looked over his shoulder at Celeste. She nodded, smiled, and lifted a hand in a wave. "See you soon," she called, and drifted back toward the gates.

"Right," he said, and his voice cracked a little. He gulped and looked at Angela. "Where are we going?"

"A little town in Ohio called Keelan Grove."

"We're going to Ohio?"

"*You* are."

"Why?"

Angela stopped and put a finger to her lips. "Listen. Do you hear that?"

Nathan listened.

There. It was that music again, the tinkling melody he'd heard when he'd first come through the gates. Only now it seemed closer, clearer.

Looking around, he saw only mist.

"What is it?" he whispered.

"It's a music box. A present from Grandma Butterfield."

"Grandma Butterfield? Who's she?"

"She's Brittany's Grandma."

"Brittany? Who's Brittany?"

Angela's eyes sparkled. "She's the baby girl who was just born to the Butterfields. Are you ready to meet her?"

Nathan hesitated only a moment, listening for the music. And now he heard another sound, even more delicate . . . the fragile *coo* of a new-born testing her tiny voice.

Nathan smiled and nodded at Angela. "I'm ready," he told her, and off he went, to become a guardian angel.

Chapter One

"Brittany! Get out of there," Beth called, pounding on the bathroom door.

"In a second," Brittany replied calmly, reaching for her hairbrush. She wiped the steam from the shower off the mirror and ran the brush through her still-damp, blondish-brown pageboy and wished, as always, that she had hair like Beth. Her older sister's long golden mane was always full of bounce and shine, instead of hanging limply like Brittany's did.

She heard another voice on the other side of the door. "She's *still* in there?" Brooke, Beth's identical twin, asked in an irritated voice.

"She keeps saying she'll be out in a second."

"This is crazy. We're going to be late." Brooke pounded on the door. "Brittany, *come on!*"

"In a second," Brittany said, reaching for her glasses and putting them on. Again, she checked her reflection in the mirror. Now that she could see a sharp, clear image, she winced. She'd definitely looked much better in soft-focus.

Why couldn't she look more like the twins, who were fifteen and gorgeous? Why did she have to have this too-round face perched on top of a chunky body? Why did she have to wear these stupid braces?

The one feature Brittany shared with her older sisters was a pair of big blue eyes inherited from their mother. But hers were hidden behind these inch-thick tortoiseshell framed glasses, and her parents wouldn't let her get contact lenses.

Money was too tight these days for "extras," and contacts fell into that category, according to Mr. Butterfield. "Besides," he was always telling Brittany, "look at me. I wear glasses, too."

Somehow, Brittany couldn't seem to make him understand that not all twelve-year-old girls wanted to be mirror images of their middle-aged fathers.

"Brittany! If you don't get out of there this instant, we're going to break the door down," Beth yelled.

Now *that* was an interesting notion. Brittany paused and contemplated letting them try it. She wondered if they could even do it—the house was over a hundred years old, and the door looked pretty solid.

"What the heck is going on up there?"

Uh-oh. That was her father's voice.

Brittany grabbed her quilted bag of hair mousses and gels and sprays—all of them useless on her blah hair, but she still kept trying— and opened the bathroom door.

"Hi, Dad," she said brightly, waving at her father, who stood there in his pajamas.

Mr. Butterfield was a police officer and, lately, he was working the night shift. That meant he came home at dawn and went to bed just as Mrs. Butterfield was getting up for her job as a bank teller.

Mr. Butterfield scowled, first at Brittany, then at Beth and Brooke, both of whom were standing there in long cotton nightgowns with their blond hair sleep-tousled.

"We didn't mean to wake you up, Dad," Beth said sweetly, then glared at Brittany. "But *she's* been hogging the bathroom for, like, an hour."

"I have not!" Brittany said. "I was only in there long enough to take a shower and dry my hair." *And experiment with makeup*, she added mentally. But that didn't count because she'd ended up washing it all off. She'd been hoping that some lipstick and eyeliner would make her look more sophisticated, but she couldn't seem to get either on straight, and ended up with lips and eyes that were rimmed in jagged lines.

Mr. Butterfield grumbled something no one could understand, and turned and headed back down the stairs to the big master bedroom on the first floor.

Beth and Brooke exchanged a glance, then both lunged toward the bathroom at the same moment, crashing into each other in the doorway.

"Brooke, come on, I was waiting longer!"

"Beth, you know I'm always really quick in there. I'll be in and out of the shower in two seconds, then you can have it all to yourself."

"No way! That's totally not fair!"

Brittany shook her head and left her sisters arguing there. She headed toward her bedroom, the last one at the end of the long hall, next to her eight-year-old sister Barbie's room.

Barbie had already left for school—Mrs. Butterfield had dropped her off at Elm Brook Elementary on the way to work.

This was the first year Brittany wouldn't be going there, too.

This year, Brittany was going to be in seventh grade, and that meant going to Keelan Grove Middle School.

And *that* meant trouble.

*   *   *

"I can't believe you're not psyched about this, Britt," Camisha Johnson said, shaking her head. The bright beads on the bottoms of her braids bobbed slightly. "I mean, how can you say you wish we were all back at Elm Brook?"

"I don't know. I just—"

"It's about time we got out of that baby place," Lacey Gibbons interrupted. She tossed her long, curly red hair and made a face. "Who wants to be in the same building with a bunch of kindergartners?"

"It's not that," Brittany told her friends, wishing she'd never opened her mouth in the first place. "I just kind of miss it, that's all."

"How can you miss it already? It's only the first day back," Camisha pointed out. "I bet after five minutes in middle school, you'll love it."

"Sure," Brittany said halfheartedly. "I bet you're right."

But as they continued walking toward their new school, she grew more and more anxious.

Elm Brook was right in her neighborhood, only a few blocks away from home. The middle school was further away, in the center of town. It would be full of strangers, kids from the five other elementary schools in town.

Brittany thought of her sixth grade class. She'd known everyone in it since kindergarten, with the exception of Lia Knowlton, a new girl whose family had moved to the neighborhood halfway through the year. Brittany remembered how Lia had been on the fringes of everything, how she had always sat alone during cookie break, reading a book.

That's how I'm going to be this year, Brittany thought miserably. She already had her schedule, and Camisha and Lacey weren't in any of her classes. They had almost every class together, though.

Brittany noticed that they were wearing similar outfits, as though they'd consulted each other before getting dressed. Camisha had on cream-colored leggings and an oversized red sweater. Lacey had on black leggings and an oversized gray sweater. They were both wearing makeup, too—a lot of makeup. Maybe too much for broad daylight, but still . . .

Brittany wished she'd left her own lipstick and eyeliner on. Maybe she could have asked one of her sisters to help her straighten the lines. And she wished she weren't wearing these baggy, faded jeans and a long-sleeved blue shirt that had seen better days. Not that she wanted to be all dressed up in some baby back-to-school frock, or anything. But she could have taken more time to figure out what to wear.

Her friends were talking about Mr. Travis, who would be their English teacher.

"My brother told me he's really tough,"

Camisha said. "You got Mrs. Paiva instead, right, Brittany? She's supposed to be this sweet old lady. You're lucky."

"Yeah," she said halfheartedly. "I guess. But don't you guys think it'll be kind of strange, changing classrooms for every subject, instead of having one teacher?"

"I think it'll be cool," Lacey said.

"Yeah, but won't you miss having one teacher who knows you really well? I mean, Ms. Dolin was great. She *loved* us," Brittany said wistfully, thinking of their sixth grade teacher.

Ms. Dolin had been the one who told Brittany she was a talented writer, and she had been the one who had encouraged Brittany to create a school newspaper last September. She had stayed after school lots of times to help Brittany print out the *Elm Brook Gazette*. And at the sixth grade graduation ceremony in June, she had awarded Brittany with a little silver pin shaped like a newspaper.

"Yeah, Ms. Dolin was cool," Camisha agreed, "but remember Mr. Belk? He was a real jerk, and we were stuck with him the whole fourth grade year. This way, with a bunch of different teachers, even if one's a loser, you only have to deal with him or her for, like, an hour each day."

"I guess," Brittany said glumly. She wished Camisha and Lacey would stop being so annoyingly optimistic. It was lonely, being the only miserable one.

Brittany thought back to fourth grade, when she and Camisha and Lacey had formed a secret Mr. Belk Haters Club. They'd had a password and a special handshake and everything.

Well, those good old days were over. There was no chance of forming a secret anti–middle school club. Brittany's two best friends were practically bouncing along the sidewalk, they were so excited about going there.

If you can't beat 'em, join 'em, popped into Brittany's head.

That was her father's favorite saying. But she might as well try it.

So she pasted on a big smile and turned to Camisha and Lacey. "Know what? I bet you guys are absolutely right. I'm probably going to *love* middle school."

Brittany *hated* middle school.

She hated everything about it. The place was too big, too confusing, too noisy, and too crowded. She'd been hoping to find some familiar faces from Elm Brook in her classes, but there were only a few—most of them boys, and no one she was particularly close to. And she was pretty much stuck with the same group in every class.

She passed Camisha and Lacey a few times in the halls that first day. They were always together, always laughing and looking like they were having a terrific time.

Which made Brittany feel even more out of it as she made her way from class to class alone, getting lost at least three times.

As the three of them walked home together after school, Brittany felt only utter relief that the day was over, and utter dread at the thought of coming back tomorrow.

Meanwhile, her friends giggled and chattered the whole way.

"My favorite class was definitely math. The teacher is so cute—I mean, he looks just like Keanu Reeves," Lacey said for the millionth time.

"He does not," Camisha protested for the millionth time. "I mean, he looks *kinda* like him, but definitely not *just* like him."

Brittany sighed.

She felt like saying, *My least favorite class was gym. The teacher, Miss Rigby, looks just like Jack Nicholson did in that movie* Wolf. *And I hated lunch period, too. I had to sit all by myself, and the food was disgusting—some kind of horrible meat in a pukey brown sauce over a wet, mushy clump of rice.*

But she didn't say it. She didn't say anything the whole way home. She was afraid that if she opened her mouth, she'd cry.

* * *

"Uh-oh," Nathan said. "Look at her, Angela. She's miserable."

"She sure is, poor thing. What are you going to do?"

"What am *I* going to do?"

"You're her guardian angel, aren't you?" Angela asked, poking him in the chest with her index finger. "Isn't it your job to take care of her?"

"Sure, but . . ." Nathan trailed off, puzzled. "I mean, I kept her from getting pulled out too far when she was swimming in the ocean during that Florida vacation, and I made sure she didn't step on broken glass with her bare feet this summer, but what am I supposed to do about this? How can I save her from . . . middle school?"

Angela shrugged. "That's up to you."

The two of them looked back at Brittany, who was just going into her bedroom. They watched as she closed the door behind her, then threw herself down on her bed and started sobbing.

Nathan looked at Angela. "Come on, Ang', help me. What can I do for her?"

"I can't tell you. If I do, you'll ruin your chances of getting your wings. You have to do this on your own."

"Great," Nathan muttered. "I don't have a clue."

Helplessly, he watched Brittany crying miserably into her pillow.

Chapter Two

Dinnertime at the Butterfields' was always a rushed, noisy affair. It had to be squeezed into the hour between when Mrs. Butterfield arrived home from her job and when Mr. Butterfield left for his.

Sometimes, Brittany wished she weren't the middle kid in a family of four girls. Barbie always got a lot of attention as the baby of the family. And Beth and Brooke got extra attention because they were the oldest, and twins. Most days, Brittany resented all of them for hogging the spotlight.

But tonight, as they all sat down at the big, scarred wooden table in the dining room, Brittany was glad to be in the background while her three sisters chattered away about school. She sat silently eating the chili her mother had made in the Crock-Pot, thinking about how miserable the next three years of her life were going to be.

And would things even get better after that? High school was probably worse than middle school. Unless you were naturally popular and beautiful, like the twins, who were bursting with excitement over their first day at Keelan Grove High.

"And you know what?" Brooke was saying. "He told me that I was crazy if I didn't go out for junior varsity cheering. He said I'd be a natural!"

"Yeah, and we both signed up to try out," Beth said. "You should see the uniforms the Jayvees get to wear . . . they're gold and blue with the cutest flared skirts."

"I signed up for something, too," Barbie put in. "I'm going to be on the safety patrol, and I get to wear a banner and a badge."

"Sounds great," Mr. Butterfield said, ruffling her dark hair. Barbie was the only Butterfield girl who had his coloring, including a pair of thick-fringed brown eyes that everyone called "puppy dog" eyes.

"How about you, Brittany?" Mrs. Butterfield asked, turning to her. "You're awfully quiet. How was your first day at middle school?"

She shrugged. "It was all right."

"Only 'all right'?" Mr. Butterfield helped himself to another piece of store-bought corn bread. "Didn't you sign up for anything? Safety patrol? Cheerleading?"

"Yeah, right, Dad," Brittany muttered. As if she could ever try out for cheerleading. She was way too lumpy and klutzy for something like that.

"Did you remember to tell Mrs. Paiva I said hi?" Beth asked.

"Uh, I forgot."

Brittany didn't bother to tell her sister that as soon as the English teacher had called her name when she was checking attendance, she'd said, *Butterfield? You're not related to the twins, Beth and Brooke, are you, dear?* As if she couldn't believe that the two swans could have such an ugly duckling as a sister.

And Brittany had felt her face turn bright red as the whole class turned around and looked at her, and all she could do was nod and mumble, "They're my sisters."

"Hey, did you get Miss Rigby for gym?" asked Brooke.

"Yeah. Why?"

"She's great. She loved me and Beth. We always got to be team captains."

"Oh." Brittany thought about how she'd instantly disliked the gym teacher. "Don't you think she kind of looks like Jack Nicholson?"

"A woman who looks like Jack Nicholson?" Mr. Butterfield shuddered. "She sounds lovely." He checked his watch and pushed back his chair. "Well, men, it's time for me to go off and fight crime."

Calling his family of females "men" was Mr. Butterfield's idea of a joke. He had a strange sense of humor.

"Take the rest of this corn bread with you, Jack," Mrs. Butterfield said, standing up and grabbing the tin foil off the table. "I'll wrap it for you." She headed for the kitchen with her husband right behind her.

"So Britt, tell us more," Beth said, pouring more water into her glass. The twins were on a health kick and only drank spring water these days.

"Yeah, did you get lost?" Brooke asked.

"No," Brittany lied.

"You're kidding. Seventh graders are notorious for getting lost in that building. It's, like, a maze." Beth sipped her water.

"Yeah," Brooke said, "And if you do get lost, don't ask an upperclassman for directions, whatever you do. They'll totally send you in the wrong direction."

"Thanks for the warning." Brittany wasn't about to tell them that she'd made that mistake already. Unable to find her Social Studies classroom, she'd asked two eighth grade girls how to get there. By the time she'd finished following the makeshift map they'd drawn, she found herself opening the door to the janitor's closet way back in a corner of the third floor.

The next two times she'd gotten lost, she'd played it safe and asked teachers where to go.

"And whatever you do, make sure you don't eat the hot lunches." That piece of sisterly advice came from Beth.

"Why not?"

"Because a few years ago, some kid found a mouse foot in the stew. He almost ate it."

Barbie squealed. "Gross!"

"You're kidding." Brittany set down her spoon and pushed her half-empty bowl of chili away.

"No, it's true, and everyone says the kid went crazy and had to drop out of school," Brooke said.

"Yeah, and last year Sydney LeBreux found a giant black hair in the spaghetti," Beth added. "Now she's anorexic."

"One time I found a hair in my ice cream at Never On Sundae," Barbie contributed. "That's why Mom doesn't like to eat there anymore."

"That was *your* hair," Brooke told her.

"Was not."

"Was so. I was there."

"Were not."

"Was, too."

This could go on all night. Brittany pushed back her chair and stood up. "Are you guys done eating?'' she asked. It was her night to clear the table.

Everyone was finished, so Brittany started stacking dishes. Barbie and Brooke took their *were not—was too* argument into the living room, but Beth lingered.

"You're going to love middle school, Brittany," she said.

"Yeah."

"You don't seem that thrilled."

"I am."

"Really?" Beth looked carefully at her. "I mean, it might be a little scary at first, to be the littlest fish in a big pond, but you'll get used to it."

"I know." Brittany wasn't in the mood for this. She picked up the stack of dishes and carried them toward the kitchen.

She hated it when her sisters tried to give her advice based on their experience. Couldn't they see that she was different? She wasn't outgoing or bubbly or pretty. She didn't have loads of friends, like they did. She only had two really good friends, who all of the sudden seemed like strangers.

Besides, the twins had each other, no matter what. They never had to do anything on their own.

Brittany had never felt so lonely in her life.

* * *

The rest of that week at school was even worse.

On Wednesday, Brittany forgot her locker combination and had to go to the office after homeroom to have it looked up. The ninth grade girl on duty there rolled her eyes when Brittany told her what she needed.

"Here," the girl said, tossing her long hair and handing over the combination scribbled on a slip of paper. "Don't lose it this time. Maybe you could have your mommy sew it inside your shirt or something."

Two ninth grade boys waiting on the bench outside the vice principal's office snickered at that, and Brittany left the office feeling like a jerk.

In gym class on Thursday, Miss Rigby announced that they would be playing softball outside. Feeling gawky and fat in her unflattering blue gym shorts and white T-shirt, Brittany stood waiting to be chosen by one of the two team captains Miss Rigby had selected. Brittany didn't know either girl, but naturally, both of them were lean, athletic, popular types. And naturally, both of them ignored Brittany and a few other unlikely prospects until everyone else had been chosen.

Finally, when only two girls were left standing on the line—Brittany and Mona, who had also gone to Elm Brook and who must have weighed over two hundred pounds—one of the captains pointed reluctantly at Brittany and said, "You."

At least I wasn't chosen last, Brittany told herself as she joined the rest of the team in jogging out onto the field. Then she had her first turn up at bat, and instinctively ducked when she saw the ball sailing toward her. She heard the rest of her teammates groan, and knew the captain wished she'd chosen Mona instead.

"What's the matter with you, Butterfield?" Miss Rigby barked from the sidelines. "You're supposed to swing the bat and hit the ball."

As if she didn't know. Fighting back humiliation, she poised the bat again and waited. This time, when the ball whizzed in her direction, she forced herself not to duck . . . even though it was heading straight for her face.

Plunk.

It smacked her in the forehead. She gasped, dropped the bat, and rubbed her head as everyone around her groaned.

"Butterfield, what are you *doing?*" Miss Rigby hollered, then tacked on an unfeeling, "Are you all right?"

"I'm fine."

"Sit down, Butterfield," the teacher ordered.

Brittany returned to the bench still rubbing

her head, conscious of the glares from her teammates, the captain, and the teacher.

She didn't think anything more miserable than that could happen, but she was wrong.

During lunch period on Friday, she got to the cafeteria early and put her book bag at the end of a table in the corner. She figured that way back here, fewer people would notice her eating alone.

She went through the line and, remembering what her sisters had said, decided not to get the hot lunch, even though it was pizza. Instead she got an ice cream drumstick and Twinkies, figuring they were prewrapped and had to be safe.

She made her way back to the spot she had saved, then stopped short. The table had been overrun with eighth grade boys. Her book bag was nowhere to be seen.

Now what?

She hovered a few feet from the table, trying to figure out what to do. She was too intimidated to walk over there and ask about her stuff. But on the other hand, how was she going to explain to her teachers that she had somehow misplaced all her textbooks? And what about her parents? They had bought her the brand new book bag as a birthday present just last month.

Finally, she decided to stop being such a baby. Straightening her shoulders and clutching her Twinkies so hard that the cream smushed out the sides, she marched over to the closest boy. He was wearing a football jersey and leaning his chair back on two legs, with his feet propped on the table next to a tray that held four slices of pizza.

"Um, excuse me," Brittany said, stopping behind him.

He either didn't hear her or was ignoring her.

She cleared her throat and spoke a little louder. "Excuse me," she said, tapping him on the shoulder.

He lost his balance and the chair went flying backward, landing on the floor with a loud bang. The boy lay sprawled at Brittany's feet.

Everyone in the cafeteria was silent for a moment. Then the table of the boy's friends erupted in hoots and whistles, and the rest of the place went crazy.

Horrified, Brittany felt her face grow hot.

"Yo, Joey, nice move. What are you gonna do as an encore?" someone asked as the boy scrambled off the floor, scowling and rubbing his back.

He glared at Brittany. "What the heck is wrong with you?"

"I . . . I'm really sorry," she said desperately, feeling dozens of pairs of eyes on her.

"Why'd you shove my chair out from under me?"

"I didn't. It was an accident. I didn't mean to

do it," she explained, aware that Joey's friends weren't going to let him live this down. They were still snickering and cracking jokes.

"An accident? What are you, a klutz?" Joey had a mean face, Brittany realized, and stopped feeling so sorry. His dark eyes were cold and he had them narrowed at her in a threatening way. And he was big—almost as big as her father.

"No, I . . . I was just going to ask you if you'd seen my book bag," she said lamely.

"Your *book bag?* Why would I have seen your book bag?"

"I left it on this table, and—"

"Big mistake," Joey said. "This table is ours. Anyone stupid enough to leave something here doesn't get it back."

Brittany didn't know what to say to that. She looked around for the cafeteria monitor. He was standing over some kid who was wiping up milk he'd spilled on the floor.

She glanced at Joey's friends. They weren't paying any attention to her now. Most of them were shoving down pizza and talking about some football game.

"Get lost," Joey said to her, sitting in his chair again and turning his back.

"But I—"

"Get lost," he repeated, not looking at her.

Brittany hesitated only a moment, then walked away. She could feel tears stinging her eyes and a lump rising in her throat, but the last thing she wanted to do was cry in front of this roomful of strangers. And no one was allowed out of the cafeteria until lunch period was over.

So there was nothing for her to do but find another spot and sit down. She slid into an empty chair at the end of a tableful of girls. They looked like ninth graders, and Brittany could have sworn they were giggling about her.

There was no way she could eat the Twinkies, which had been reduced to mush, and she didn't want the ice cream drumstick anymore either. But she had to do something, so she gingerly unwrapped it and nibbled at it until it was so melted and messy that she had to throw it away.

Then there was nothing to do but sit there, ignore the giggling girls a few seats away, and pray for the bell to ring.

"Look at her, sitting there alone. She's not doing very well, is she," Nathan commented to Angela.

"No, she isn't." Angela shrugged. "Poor kid."

"I've got to do something," Nathan said. "I can't stand it. But I just don't know how I can help. This is complicated."

Angela shrugged. "It is, but you're her guardian angel, Nathan. It's up to you to figure something out."

"I know . . ."

He straightened his baseball cap and continued to watch Brittany. She looked so forlorn, sitting all by herself in the midst of so many other kids, most of them in groups, laughing and eating and chattering.

"What she needs is a new friend," Nathan decided abruptly.

"That would be a start," Angela told him.

"I think I have an idea." Nathan rubbed his chin thoughtfully as a plan began to formulate in his head.

Chapter Three

On Saturday morning, Camisha's mother dropped the three girls off at the mall. As she walked through the wide corridor with her friends, Brittany could almost pretend things were back to normal.

"I *have* to find that pair of earrings again," Lacey said. "I can't believe I didn't buy them last week. I *knew* they would go with that shirt I want to borrow from my sister. Now I can't even remember which store they were in."

"Express, wasn't it?" Camisha asked. "I could swear it was Express."

"I don't know . . . I thought it was The Limited," Brittany said.

"Was it?" Lacey shrugged. "We'll have to try both."

"Maybe I'll get some earrings, too," Camisha said. She reached up and patted her double-pierced lobes. She was wearing two pairs of dangling gold earrings.

"Hey, Britt," Lacey suggested, "why don't you get your ears done today?"

"I don't think so." Brittany wasn't about to tell her friends that her parents were making her wait until she turned thirteen to get her ears pierced. She knew Lacey and Camisha would roll their eyes and joke about yet another crazy "Butterfield Rule." They both thought Brittany's parents were old-fashioned and strict.

Camisha's parents, who were both college professors, were really liberal and laid-back. And Lacey's mom, who was divorced from her dad, was hardly ever around. She always seemed to be either working or out on dates.

Brittany noted that both Lacey and Camisha were wearing makeup again today. In her opinion, Lacey had on way too much eye shadow. And Camisha's milk-chocolate colored skin was highlighted with an unnaturally bright shade of blush.

And they looked kind of silly, both wearing jeans and boots and sweaters when it was over eighty degrees outside.

Brittany was wearing shorts, sneakers, and a baggy T-shirt. And she still hadn't gotten around to asking Beth or Brooke to show her how to put on makeup. She promised herself she would find out before Monday.

"Hey, Camisha!" someone called from the other side of the corridor.

The three girls stopped and looked around.

"It's Jerry," Lacey squealed, jabbing Camisha in the ribs and pointing. "And Quent is with him."

"Who are they?" Brittany asked, watching as the two boys made their way over.

"The black one is Jerry Rogerson—his locker is near mine, and Camisha's in love with him," Lacey said, and giggled.

Camisha giggled, too. "I am not. You're in love with Quent."

"So?" Lacey poked her and said, "Shhh, they're right there."

The boys stopped a few feet away. Both were well-built and wearing Keelan Grove Middle School football jackets.

"Yo, what's up?" asked the one who had "Quent" embroidered on his jacket.

"Not much," Lacey said. She giggled again.

"You guys been here long?" Jerry asked, swinging his plastic Foot Locker bag over his shoulder.

"I don't know, have we?" Camisha asked, sounding giddy.

"Seems like it. This place is, like, *sooo* boring," Lacey said, rolling her eyes.

Brittany wondered what had gotten into her. And Camisha, too. They were both acting so crazy all of a sudden, tossing their hair around and giggling.

"Yeah, this place rots," Camisha said.

Brittany frowned slightly. It had been her friends' idea to come here. They were always talking about how much they loved this mall.

"Yeah, we need a *real* mall around here," Quent said. "This place doesn't even have a food court."

"Oh, wow, I *love* food courts. They're, like, great!"

That had come from Lacey.

Brittany was getting annoyed with this whole conversation. For one thing, her friends were acting like idiots. For another, they were acting like she didn't even exist. They practically had their backs turned on her.

Then Jerry looked over Camisha's shoulder and said, "Hey, aren't you the one who shoved Joey Kulaga onto the floor in the cafeteria during second lunch yesterday?"

Everyone looked at Brittany.

"I didn't *shove* him," she said lamely. "It was an accident."

"Yeah, well, he's not very happy about it," Quent said, shaking his head.

Both Camisha and Lacey were wide-eyed, their mouths hanging open.

"Brittany, that was *you?*" Camisha asked. "I

heard some seventh grade girl had a run-in with Joey, but I can't believe it was you!"

"Yeah, I heard it, too. Everyone was talking about it yesterday during last period," Lacey said. "Everyone says Joey's out to get you now."

Brittany felt her knees weaken and her stomach lurch, and for a moment she was afraid she was going to throw up, or pass out, right in the middle of the mall.

"He's out to *get* me?" she repeated. "Why?"

"Because he's Joey Kulaga, that's why," Jerry said. "You don't mess with him."

"He's on the team with us, and he's a tough dude," Quent added. "Man, I'm glad I'm not you."

Most people are, Brittany thought.

She looked from Quent to Jerry. Both of them were shaking their heads, like she was a goner. And Camisha and Lacey still looked shocked.

"Do you really think he'll come after me?" Brittany asked in a small voice.

"Definitely," Camisha said cheerfully. "I heard he once bashed some kid so hard he knocked two of his teeth out, and that was just because he wouldn't let Joey cheat off him during a test."

"I heard that, too," Quent said. "But I heard the kid *did* let him cheat, and Joey hit him because he still didn't pass the test."

Brittany chewed her lower lip.

Lacey looked at her and asked, "Wow, what are you going to do, Britt?"

"I have no idea." She took a deep breath and let it out shakily.

"Maybe you should start wearing a helmet and mouth guard to school," Jerry suggested, and everyone but Brittany laughed.

"Yeah, or a suit of armor," Quent said.

That really made the four of them crack up.

They continued making jokes for a few minutes while Brittany stood there feeling half-embarrassed, half-terrified.

Finally, Jerry said he and Quent had to get going. Camisha and Lacey were obviously disappointed.

"See you at school on Monday," Camisha called after them.

"Yeah, see you Monday," Lacey echoed.

As soon as the boys were out of earshot, Lacey and Camisha burst into excited chatter, analyzing everything they had said and done.

"Did you see the way Jerry raised his eyebrow at me when he asked how long we'd been here?" Camisha asked. "Wasn't that adorable? What do you think it means?"

"I have no idea, but did you see Quent maneuvering to stand closer to me when they first showed up?" Lacey sounded hopeful. "I mean, I think that was what he was doing, don't you?"

"Definitely," Camisha assured her. "Jerry's so cute, isn't he? What do you think, Brittany?"

"Uh huh," she said absently, her mind on Joey Kulaga.

"How about Quent? What did you think about him?" Lacey asked. "You don't think he's too short for me, do you?"

"Uh huh," Brittany said.

"Britt! Did you even hear a word I said?" Lacey sounded annoyed.

"What? Sorry." Brittany looked at her friends. "You guys, what am I going to do?"

They both shrugged, looking bored with the Joey issue now that Quent and Jerry were gone.

"It's no big deal," Camisha said blandly.

"Yeah, he probably won't even do anything to you."

"But what if he does?"

Her friends shrugged again.

Then Lacey turned to Camisha. "Where do you think those guys went? Do you think they left?"

"I don't know. Maybe they're still around someplace. They went toward that end of the mall. I bet they went to McDonald's. Come on, let's go," Camisha said.

Lacey giggled. "What are we going to do, follow them around?"

"If we bump into them again," Camisha said,

giggling, too, "we can just be like, wow, what a surprise!"

Brittany sighed and checked her watch. Her mother wasn't picking them up for another two hours.

There was nothing to do but tag along with Lacey and Camisha, wondering when and why they had turned into total strangers.

And worry about what Joey Kulaga was going to do to her.

And wish she had never been born.

First thing Monday morning in English class, Mrs. Paiva asked everyone to open their textbooks. Brittany groaned inwardly. Her English book had been in the bag that had vanished from the cafeteria Friday afternoon.

Naturally, Mrs. Paiva noticed immediately that she wasn't turning to page twenty-six like everyone else. "Brittany?" she asked from the front of the room. "Is there a problem?"

She felt everyone looking at her as she cleared her throat and said, "I, um, forgot my book. I'm sorry."

Mrs. Paiva smiled. "That's all right, dear. You can share with someone else. Kara? Would you kindly allow Brittany to look on with you?"

The girl across from her, Kara Raposo, obediently slid her desk across the aisle. Brittany didn't know her but she was in most of her classes.

"Hey, I saw the deal with Joey in the cafeteria the other day," Kara said in a low voice as Mrs. Paiva grasped a stick of chalk in her arthritic fingers and started writing a sentence on the board. "What are you going to do?"

Brittany shrugged.

"You do know he's out to get you," Kara said, sounding like she thought Brittany was a little slow or something.

Brittany shrugged again. What was she supposed to say?

At the end of class, Mrs. Paiva assigned several pages of exercises as homework. Brittany knew she was going to have to ask for a new book for this class and for Social Studies and Math.

And what about the rest of the stuff that had been in her book bag? The keys to her house, and all her notebooks and folders and pens and stuff? And what about the book bag itself?

Her parents would demand to know how she could have lost everything. And she couldn't tell them the truth. They would probably go to the principal or something, and then Brittany would be in an even bigger mess.

Miserably, she made her way from class to class.

When lunchtime arrived, she knew she

couldn't go to the cafeteria and risk a run-in with Joey Kulaga. There was just no way.

But what else could she do?

If only she could find a place to sit and read until lunch period was over. But you weren't allowed to go into the library—which everyone called the media center—unless you had a pass from a teacher. You weren't allowed to leave the building, either—the doors were locked while classes were in session. And you couldn't just roam the halls, because teachers and hall monitors patrolled them.

Brittany felt like she was in prison.

Wasn't there *anyplace* where she could . . .

The auditorium!

It would be empty. And as far as she knew, it wasn't used for anything but assemblies, and drama club practice after school.

She hurried down to the first floor and arrived in front of the auditorium just as the bell rang. After looking around quickly to make sure no one was watching, she opened one of the double doors and slipped through, pulling it quietly closed behind her.

It took a moment for her eyes to adjust to the dim lighting.

And as soon as they did, she realized, with a stab of panic, that she wasn't alone.

Chapter Four

He was sitting on the edge of the stage down at the front of the room. From where Brittany stood, she thought he seemed older than a ninth grader, but you never knew. He looked pretty tall, and had a lanky build. He wore faded jeans, a long-sleeved navy T-shirt, and a navy baseball cap. His high-top-sneaker-clad feet dangled against the side of the stage casually. He was leaning back on his hands, and seemed to be chewing gum.

He was the picture of nonchalance, but something told Brittany that he didn't just happen to be here.

"Hi," he said, almost like he'd been expecting her.

Which, of course, he couldn't possibly have been doing. Because she hadn't known she was even coming in here until a few minutes ago, when the idea had popped into her head.

"What's up?" the boy asked, his voice bouncing off the walls of the empty auditorium.

Brittany took a step backward and reached behind her to open the door and get out of here before . . .

"Wait!" the boy called out, pushing himself off the stage with a quick thrust of his hands. "You're Brittany, right? Brittany Butterfield?"

She froze when he said her name.

How did he know her? Who was he? Some hit man Joey Kulaga had hired to bump her off?

He started up the aisle toward her, and Brittany felt panic sweeping over her. She was afraid to move . . . and afraid not to. But she couldn't have if she wanted to. It was as if her legs had taken root in the scarred gray tile floor, and she was powerless to react in any way as the boy drew closer.

"Hey, relax," he said, stopping a few feet away. "You look terrified. I'm not going to hurt you."

All hit men probably said that to their victims, Brittany thought vaguely.

And yet, he didn't look like a hit man. His dark eyes had an earnest, serious expression, and even in this dim light Brittany could make out the freckles sprinkled across his nose.

It was the freckles that did it. Somehow, she

just couldn't believe that a boy who had freckles on his nose was her enemy.

She let go of the door handle she'd been gripping behind her, and found her voice. "How did you know my name?" she asked, and it came out a little squeaky.

He shrugged. "I'm Nathan," was all he said in response.

"Nathan . . . ?" she repeated, waiting for his last name, but he just nodded.

"I think I have something of yours, Brittany," he said, smiling.

"You think you have something of mine?" She sounded idiotic, repeating everything he said, but she couldn't seem to help it.

Nathan just smiled and beckoned her to come with him. She followed him down the sloping center aisle and across the front row of seats. Then she stopped and watched while he bent down and reached under a chair.

"Is this yours?" he asked, pulling something out and holding it up.

"My book bag! Where did you get it?"

"I found it," he said, handing it over.

She hugged it, a sense of relief and gratitude washing over her. "Thank you so much," she told Nathan.

"No problem."

He watched while she unzipped the bag and

quickly scanned the contents to make sure nothing was missing.

It was all there, and she rezipped it and looked again at Nathan. "Do you go to school here?" she asked, suddenly feeling shy.

"Nope. I'm seventeen," he told her, and reached up and straightened the visor of his baseball cap. She saw that it was emblazoned with a white, overlapping N-Y.

"You're a New York Yankees fan?" she asked him, pointing at it.

"Yup." He looked pleased that she'd noticed. "They're the greatest."

"My dad likes the Indians."

He shrugged. "They're all right. But the Yankees are the American classic. They've had the greatest players—Babe Ruth, Lou Gehrig, Roger Maris, Thurman Munson . . ."

Brittany looked blankly at him.

"You don't know much about the Yankees, do you?" Nathan asked her, interrupting his happy rundown of the players.

She shook her head. "I don't know much about baseball, period. I stink at sports."

Nathan actually looked sympathetic, which was surprising, because Brittany knew most boys had no patience with a girl who wasn't good at sports.

"I can show you how to hit, if you want," he offered.

"How to hit?"

"How to hit a ball. You know, with a bat."

For a moment, Brittany was too stunned to reply. When she did manage, her voice sounded squeaky again. "Did you hear about what happened to me in gym the other day?"

He hesitated. "What do you mean?"

"How I got hit in the face with the softball?"

"Uh, no, I didn't know about *that*," he said.

But something told Brittany he did. He probably knew about Joey Kulaga, too.

Who was he, anyway? Why would he offer to teach her how to hit a ball?

"Why are you being so nice?" she asked him before she had a chance to stop and think. It came out loud and blunt, and she immediately felt herself blush.

Nathan just looked amused. "Because I'm a nice guy," he said simply.

She nodded. She believed him. He *was* a nice guy. But even so, why would a nice seventeen-year-old guy want to spend any amount of time with a dumpy, clumsy seventh-grader?

She was about to ask him that when he said, "Okay, listen, I have to get going now. I'll meet you after school tomorrow and we'll practice hitting."

"Where?"

"How about Madison Park?"

"That's only two blocks from my house."

"Is it?" he asked, not looking all that surprised. "That's good. I'll meet you by the fountain at three-thirty."

"What if it's raining?"

"It won't be."

"How do you know?"

"Uh . . . weather report," he replied, then nodded and started up the center aisle, toward the double doors. "See you then, Brittany."

"See you then." She was back to echoing him.

She watched as he slipped out into the hall. The door closed quietly behind him, leaving her alone in the quiet auditorium.

Alone and amazed.

She spent the rest of the lunch period sitting in a chair, clutching her book bag and going over and over what had just happened.

When the bell rang and she headed for her next class, she felt better than she had in a week.

"Hey, Angela," Nathan called, "Wait up!"

She turned around and broke into a smile. "Hi."

"Well?" he asked, stopping next to her.

"Well, what?"

"What did you think?"

"About what?"

"About what I did for Brittany."

"Oh, *that*."

But he saw the twinkle in her eye and knew she was teasing him.

"You did a nice job," Angela said, reaching up and giving his shoulder a pat. "What next?"

"You heard. I teach her how to hit a softball."

"And then?"

He shrugged. "I'm not sure. I mean, maybe she'll be fine then."

"Maybe." But Angela looked doubtful.

"And if she *isn't* fine, I'll keep helping her until she is. I mean, that's what I'm here for, right? That's what a guardian angel does. So where are you going now?" he asked, falling into step beside her.

"I thought I'd peek in on the Yankee game. Want to come?"

"Are you kidding?" Nathan gave her a broad grin and a thumbs-up. "But Angela, are you sure we can't give the Yanks a little nudge in the right direction if they're losing? I mean, it seems like a waste of all these special powers not to—"

"Nathan! You know the rules. Don't even think about it."

He sighed. "Okay, okay, I won't."

And together, he and Angela headed for the Bronx.

Tuesday morning in English, Mrs. Paiva told the class that an eighth grade boy, Dustin Plumb, would be coming in to make a special announcement.

Brittany saw Kara Raposo lean across the aisle toward her friend Jade Hoover. "Dustin Plumb—he's that geek who dropped the milk in the cafeteria the other day," she said, and both girls giggled.

Brittany decided she didn't like either of them, and that she felt sorry for poor Dustin Plumb, whoever he was.

Mrs. Paiva told them to take out their textbooks and turn to chapter three. As Brittany pulled hers out of her book bag, she again thought of Nathan. He had been on her mind pretty much constantly ever since yesterday afternoon. She hadn't told Camisha or Lacey what had happened, even though she knew they'd both be impressed by the fact that she'd had an actual conversation with a high school boy. For some reason, she wanted to keep Nathan to herself.

There was a knock on the classroom door, and Mrs. Paiva went over to answer it.

"Dustin!" she said warmly. "Come on in."

He *did* look like a geek, Brittany thought reluctantly. He was painfully thin, with long, knobby white arms sticking out below the short sleeves of the striped polo shirt that hung on his frame. He had too-short, too-neat dark hair, thick glasses, and pointy features. And he looked incredibly nervous, as he planted himself in front of Mrs. Paiva's desk.

"Everyone, this is Dustin Plumb," she said, resting a proud hand on his narrow shoulder. "He's the editor of the school newspaper, the *Keelan Khronicle*. Please give him your attention."

Dustin cleared his throat and started talking.

"We can't hear you," Troy Duboff said loudly from the back of the room.

That's because you're rustling papers and snapping your gum, on purpose, Brittany thought.

"Sorry," Dustin said, clearing his throat and starting again.

"Still can't hear you," Troy said, after snapping his gum again, and a few people laughed, which made Dustin blush furiously.

"Troy," Mrs. Paiva said sternly, "please come forward and dispose of that bubblegum. Then sit quietly and you'll be able to hear."

"No problem," Troy said, strolling to the front of the room and making a big show of depositing a giant pink wad of gum in the wastepaper basket.

Brittany decided she couldn't stand him.

She focused on Dustin and gave him what she hoped was an encouraging smile. He didn't see her, though. He was staring at his shoes.

"All right, Dustin," Mrs. Paiva prompted. "Go ahead."

He took a deep breath. "I'm here to, um, invite you to write for the *Khronicle*. We need, um, reporters to do feature articles and news and sports pieces."

"Thank you, Dustin," Mrs. Paiva said, patting him on the back. She looked at the class. "Is anyone interested?"

Brittany glanced around. She wanted to raise her hand, but not if no one else was going to. And they weren't. Most of them looked bored, and Kara and Jade were whispering about something.

"Oh, come on," said Mrs. Paiva. "I'm sure that we must have quite a few budding writers here."

Brittany wished she were the kind of girl who could raise her hand and say that she was a budding writer. Hadn't she put together a monthly newspaper last year at Elm Brook? Hadn't Mrs. Dolin told her she'd done a great job, and suggested that she write for the newspaper next year in middle school?

But she just couldn't volunteer in front of everyone.

"I'm sorry, Dustin," Mrs. Paiva said. "It looks like we don't have any volunteers this period. Come on back to my fourth period class, and we'll see if anyone is interested in that group."

Dustin nodded and made a beeline for the door.

As soon as it closed behind him, Brittany heard someone—probably Troy—say "What a loser" in a voice too low for Mrs. Paiva to hear, but loud enough to make everyone snicker.

Everyone but Brittany, who slid down in her seat and wished once again that she were a different kind of person.

Chapter Five

Madison Park was fairly large, but there was only one fountain. In the center of it was a smiling cherub who always seemed to Brittany to be frolicking on the water. As Brittany hurried toward it after dashing home to change her clothes, she felt jittery.

What if Nathan wasn't there?

What if he'd been a figment of her imagination?

She'd been wondering that ever since yesterday afternoon, but every time she was about to convince herself that she'd made up the whole thing, she remembered her book bag.

It was proof that he really did exist.

But that didn't mean he was going to show up today in the park. He could have decided that he had better things to do than teach a wimpy twelve-year-old girl how to hit a softball.

Besides, Brittany didn't even *want* to learn how to hit a softball. She'd never had any desire to play sports. Her father was always saying that she was the bookworm of the family. He and Mrs. Butterfield liked to ski and play tennis. The twins were into cheerleading and gymnastics, and Barbie was the star of her ballet class. But Brittany, who had tried all of those things and failed miserably, was content to curl up with a book instead.

Not that it wouldn't be nice not to dread gym class for the next few years. Today had been horrible. Miss Rigby had taken them outside to play softball again, and this time, Brittany had been the last one chosen for a team.

All she could think about, when she found herself up at bat and that hard white ball was sailing through the air in her direction, was how much she wanted to hit it . . . and how much it would hurt if it hit her again. At the last second, she had instinctively ducked, and was instantly met with groans from her teammates, cheers from the opposition, and Miss Rigby's disgusted, "Butterfield, what's *wrong* with you?"

Maybe, Brittany thought hopefully now as she rounded the curving path that led toward the fountain, *even if Nathan can't teach me how to hit a home run or anything, he can show me how not to be afraid of the ball.*

If Nathan showed up at all.

He probably wouldn't.

But he *had* seemed like a nice guy. And a nice guy wouldn't promise to do something, and then not do it.

Well then, he probably had forgotten all about it, Brittany told herself, trying to be realistic so she wouldn't be disappointed.

She took a deep breath and looked ahead.

There was the fountain.

There was the frolicking cherub.

And there was Nathan.

"Okay, one more time, Brittany. Head up, bat ready . . ." Nathan wound and pitched.

Brittany concentrated, the way he'd taught her. She positioned herself, and when the ball was in the right spot, she swung . . . and missed.

"Steerike!" Nathan called in an un-Nathan-like voice, then added, "But not bad. Want to call it a day?"

"Definitely. I'm wiped out." She walked toward where he was standing in the center of a small clearing in a remote corner of the park. He'd told her he'd chosen this spot so she wouldn't be distracted, and in the entire time they'd been here, not a single person had come along the path.

Brittany almost wished someone had. She wouldn't have minded if Kara Raposo or someone from school happened to come by and see her hanging around with someone like Nathan.

"You should get home for supper," Nathan said, checking his watch. "It's after five."

"Is it? You're right, I'd better get going." She handed him his bat and the Yankee cap he'd given her so she could keep the sun out of her eyes while she was hitting.

"You did a really good job, Brittany," Nathan told her, and she felt pride bubble up inside at his praise.

They started walking along the path toward the park entrance.

"But I didn't even get a single hit," she pointed out. "My bat never even touched the ball, except that one time when I swung and hit the ball backward into my shoulder." She reached up and rubbed the sore spot.

"Are you okay?" he asked.

"Yeah, I'm fine. It doesn't hurt that bad. And at least I'm not ducking anymore. And the ball didn't hit me in the head again. Now maybe gym class won't be such a nightmare."

"You're getting there. You'll see," Nathan said confidently. "Any day now, I'll bet you'll get a hit."

"Bet I won't."

"Let's shake on that," he said, and held out his hand.

She grasped it and they shook. His skin felt

warm and his grip was strong and reassuring. She hated to let go.

"Nathan?" she asked as they continued along the path.

"Yeah?"

"It was really nice of you to meet me today. You're the first person who's been—well, nice to me, lately. And I really appreciate it."

"No problem. I'll meet you again on Thursday and we'll work on your batting some more."

"But you don't have to," she protested, fighting back the excitement she felt. "I mean, you probably have better things to do."

"Not really," he said, and smiled at her. "This was fun."

"It *was* fun. I never thought I'd have fun doing anything athletic."

"Well, life is full of surprises."

It sure is, she thought.

They had arrived at a fork in the path, in front of the fountain. "Here's where we separate—I go this way," Nathan said, pointing. "And you go that way."

"How'd you know?"

"Lucky guess. So I'll meet you here on Thursday—same time, same place."

"Okay," Brittany said happily.

"See you, Brittany. Have a good night." Nathan headed down the path.

"You, too. And thanks for everything, Nathan!" He waved, and Brittany watched until he'd disappeared around a curve among the trees.

Then she headed home for supper, practically skipping the whole way.

"Hey, what's in the bag?" Camisha asked Brittany Friday morning as they walked to school.

"This?" Brittany crumpled the brown paper sack more tightly closed, as if that could make it less noticeable. "Nothing."

"Nothing?" Now Lacey was looking at it, too.

Brittany wished she'd thought to stuff it into her book bag before leaving the house. But she'd been too preoccupied, thinking about Nathan. They'd met in the park again yesterday afternoon, and she'd actually hit the softball. Just once, and only a few feet before it plopped to the ground, but Nathan had been really excited about it, and so had she.

"It's just . . . a sandwich," she told her friends, unzipping her book bag now and sticking the paper bag inside. "And an apple."

"Lunch?" Camisha asked. "How come you're bringing it?"

"Because the school lunches are totally gross, that's how come. My sisters told me that people have found all kinds of disgusting things in the food there. Like bugs and rodents and stuff."

"So?" Lacey said blandly. "Everyone knows about that. But you don't have to get the hot lunch. They sell ice cream and chips and stuff in the caf, too." Lately she had developed an irritating habit of abbreviating everything—caf for cafeteria, KG for Keelan Grove. She obviously thought she was being cool, but it sounded really stupid, in Brittany's opinion.

And Brittany wasn't about to tell her friends that she no longer ate in the "caf." She could just imagine what they'd say if they knew that she'd taken to hiding in the auditorium every day during lunch period, so she wouldn't have to face Joey Kulaga.

So far, she'd been lucky. She hadn't bumped into him anywhere, and no one had mentioned him to her all week. Maybe the whole thing had blown over. But just to be on the safe side, Brittany wasn't going to set foot in the cafeteria ever again.

"So, Camisha," Lacey said, moving on to what was obviously a more interesting subject. "What did you decide to wear tonight?"

"The black jacket, definitely. And the jeans."

"What's tonight?" Brittany asked, and saw her friends exchange a glance.

"We have a date," Lacey said, like she was

trying to seem casual, but Brittany could hear a giddy note in her voice.

"A *date?*" Brittany looked at Camisha, who nodded. "You guys have a *date?*"

"We're doubling," Lacey said. "I'm going with Quent, she's going with Jerry."

"Going where?"

"To this party. At a ninth grader's house," Camisha added, obviously impressed with herself and Lacey.

Brittany only nodded. Suddenly, she forgot about Nathan and hitting the ball and Joey Kulaga and everything. All she could think was that her friends were leaving her behind. They were moving on without her, to double dates and parties and who knew what else.

And they were the only friends she had.

"So I'll come over to your house to get ready," Camisha was saying to Lacey, "and they'll pick us up there, right?"

"Right. My mother's going out at seven, so don't come before that."

The rest of the way to school, Brittany walked in silence, chewing on her lower lip while Lacey and Camisha giggled and plotted their big night out.

When the three of them got inside the building, Brittany's friends bid her a quick goodbye, then headed off to their lockers, which were in the same hallway on the first floor.

Brittany climbed the stairs alone to her locker on the second floor. She was so absorbed in her misery that she wasn't watching where she was going, and smacked right into someone as she rounded a corner at the top of the stairs.

"Oops, sorry," she said, flustered.

"It's okay," a vaguely familiar voice replied.

She looked up and saw Dustin Plumb, the newspaper editor.

"Oh . . . hi," she said, then realized he wouldn't know who she was.

Even so, he seemed surprised, then pleased. "Hi."

"I'm Brittany." It was the logical thing to say next.

"I'm Dustin."

They both nodded.

Bring up the Khronicle, Brittany commanded herself. *Tell him you want to write for it.*

But somehow, she couldn't get the thought from her brain to her lips.

And after a moment, Dustin shrugged and said, "Well, see you," and vanished into the crowd of students.

You idiot! Brittany scolded herself. *There goes your one chance to write for the school newspaper.*

But then, as she walked toward her locker, she thought, *Oh well. You probably wouldn't have been any good at it, anyway.*

*   *   *

On Saturday night, Brittany picked at her supper, trying not to think about the fact that neither Camisha nor Lacey had called her today —but unable to think of anything else. The three of them always did something together on Saturdays—the mall, or a movie, or something.

Brittany wondered about their double date last night. She wondered if maybe they had tried to call her today, but gotten a busy signal, since the twins were always tying up the line and Mr. Butterfield refused to install the call-waiting service. But they would have called back, wouldn't they? Brittany wondered about that, too.

She felt abandoned.

After dinner, she found herself in the kitchen with Beth. Her sister was loading the dishwasher while she wiped down the stove and counters.

Mr. and Mrs. Butterfield had just left for a movie, Barbie was sleeping over one of her friend's houses, and Brooke was on the phone in the living room, talking to someone named Wes.

"Who is he, anyway?" Brittany asked Beth as they heard Brooke, whose voice sounded unnaturally high, giggling and saying, "Oh, stop it, Wes, I do not!"

"He's just this guy she likes. He's a senior," Beth added.

"A senior? So he'd be, like, seventeen, right?"

"I guess."

Brittany thought about that. Then, even though the last thing she wanted was her sister prying into her life, she found herself saying, "Beth?"

"Yeah?"

"Do you know a lot of seniors?"

"Yup," Beth said, looking pleased with herself.

"And the ones you don't know personally—I mean, you'd probably recognize them by name, right?"

"Pretty much. Unless they're nobodies."

Brittany, knowing she herself was probably considered a nobody at middle school, let that slide by.

She took a deep breath and asked her sister, "Do you know a guy named Nathan?"

"Nathan who?"

"I don't know, but he's seventeen." Brittany hadn't been able to bring herself to ask his last name, or anything else, the last time she'd seen him. They'd mostly talked about softball.

"And he goes to Keelan Grove High?" Beth asked.

"I guess. I mean, it's the only high school in town."

"Nathan Timberson?" Beth asked, rearranging the dishes in the bottom rack to make room for a platter. "He's a senior."

"Is he tall and kind of thin, but not skinny, with wavy dark hair and freckles on his nose? And does he always wear a Yankee cap?"

"No, he's short and kind of stocky, with blond hair," Beth said, straightening and closing the dishwasher.

"Oh. Wrong Nathan."

"Is your Nathan cute?"

Brittany thought it over briefly. "Yeah. He is."

"Oh, really?" Beth looked intrigued. "Let me think . . . no, I guess I don't know any other Nathans."

"Oh, well . . ." Brittany tossed the sponge into the sink and headed for the back stairs.

"Britt?" her sister called after her.

"Yeah?"

"So who's this cute Nathan of the Yankee cap?"

"Just . . . nobody."

"Nobody?"

"A friend of mine."

"You've been hanging around with a cute seventeen-year-old guy," her sister said, like she didn't believe it.

"Yeah," Brittany said, "I have."

And as she climbed the stairs, she thought, *And he might just be my one and only friend in the world.*

Chapter Six

On Monday morning, Lacey and Camisha were waiting on the corner as usual.

Brittany was half relieved to see them there, and half sorry. She didn't know how she should act, or whether to confront them about not calling her over the weekend. If they hadn't waited for her today, she wouldn't have to deal with it. She could just stop speaking to them and their friendship would be over, just like that.

Now things were more complicated.

"Hey, Britt," Lacey called as she approached.

"What's up?" Camisha asked.

"Hi. Not much," Brittany said, shrugging. She noticed that they were both wearing makeup, as usual, and that their outfits were similar, as usual. Lacey had on a navy cardigan sweater, short plaid wool skirt, and tights, and

Camisha had on a peach cardigan sweater, short plaid wool skirt, and tights.

"Have a good weekend?" Lacey asked Brittany as the three of them started down the street toward school.

"I guess."

"That's good," Camisha said.

There was a pause. Out of the corner of her eye, Brittany saw the two of them exchange a glance.

"So what'd you do?" Lacey asked, kicking a stone along the sidewalk.

"Over the weekend?"

"Yeah."

"Not much," Brittany told her shortly.

She wondered if Lacey was waiting for her to ask how the double date had gone. Probably. Well, she couldn't care less about their stupid date.

Suddenly, she felt more angry than hurt. So angry that she didn't care what they thought of her.

She stopped walking, looked directly at them, and spoke without thinking. "How come you guys didn't call me on Saturday?"

They stopped, too, and looked surprised.

They couldn't have been more surprised than Brittany was. She hadn't planned on confronting them. Now what was she supposed to do? Why had she opened her mouth?

"I tried," Camisha said smoothly, after only the slightest hesitation, "but the phone was busy."

"Yeah, me, too. You really need to get your dad to put in call-waiting, Britt," Lacey advised, flipping her hair.

Brittany looked from her to Camisha. Were they telling the truth?

Why would they lie? asked a voice in the back of her mind. *They're your friends.*

She wanted to ask why they hadn't called back if the line was busy, but she was afraid to. What if they squirmed and made excuses? That would be even worse than having them come right out and tell her that they hadn't wanted to hang around with her this weekend.

She made a quick decision. The only thing to do was give them the benefit of the doubt and drop the whole thing.

"You know my dad," she said, trying to sound casual. She started walking again. "He says call-waiting is an unnecessary expense."

"Yeah, my mom used to say that, too," Lacey said. "But then she missed out on going to a Grateful Dead concert with some guy she really liked because she was on the phone with some other guy while he was trying to reach her. She ordered call-waiting the next day."

"Your mom is wild, Lacey," Camisha said. "My mom's probably never even heard of the

Grateful Dead. She only likes classical music. How about your mom, Brittany?''

"My mom? She likes stuff from when she was a teenager—like Barry Manilow and Peter Frampton."

"Peter who?" Lacey asked.

Brittany shrugged. "Some seventies guy, I guess.''

As they walked the rest of the way to school, she and Lacey and Camisha compared notes on how strange their parents were. It felt good to be included again. It was almost like old times, except . . .

Except that Brittany couldn't quite forget how abandoned they'd made her feel. Not just over the weekend, but ever since the school year had begun. It wasn't anything they'd *said*—at least, not to her face.

Brittany wondered if they talked about her when she wasn't around. What would they say? *That Brittany—what a loser. Who wants to hang around with someone who doesn't fit in?*

"See you later, Britt," Lacey said casually as they parted ways inside the school.

"Yeah, we'll meet you by your locker later to walk home," Camisha said.

Then, with a wave, they headed off together, as usual.

But something told Brittany that even though things might seem all right again on the surface, things had changed between her and her friends.

Maybe for good.

On Tuesday after school, Brittany rushed home to change, then hurried over to the park to meet Nathan.

He was waiting in their usual spot, reading a copy of *Yankee Magazine*. He folded it and tucked it into his jeans pocket when he saw Brittany.

"Hi!" he said cheerfully.

"Hi, Nathan." She felt relieved to see him. She kept expecting him to not show up, but he always did. And he always seemed happy to be with her.

"You ready?" he asked, picking up the bat and ball.

"You bet."

They started walking toward the isolated clearing.

"Nathan?" Brittany asked shyly.

"Yeah?"

"Do you go to Keelan Grove High?"

Was it her imagination, or did he suddenly look uncomfortable? But he answered with a smooth, "Sure do." Then he swung the bat playfully in front of him as they walked, and said,

"Hey, did I ever tell you why Reggie Jackson is my all-time favorite Yankee?"

"I don't think so . . ."

"You're kidding. I didn't? I never told you that Reggie hit *three* home runs in one game of the '78 World Series?"

"Wow," Brittany said, trying to sound impressed.

"It was the coolest thing," Nathan told her. "I had made a bet with my dad before that game. I said Reggie was going to hit a home run, and my dad said he wasn't. You should have seen dad when he hit *three*. That was some game."

"I bet it was," Brittany murmured, and he went on talking about it, describing each play of the game in loving detail.

But Brittany's mind wasn't on the World Series. She was trying to figure out how to find out Nathan's last name and where he lived. It seemed awkward and bold just to come right out and ask him. What if he said "Why do you want to know?"

Well, why do *you want to know?* she asked herself.

It didn't really matter, did it?

It was just . . . well, there was something kind of—strange about Nathan. He seemed too good to be true. Too good to be *real*.

And when she wasn't with him, she kept finding herself wondering if he wasn't just a figment of her imagination.

She glanced at him as they arrived in the clearing and he handed her the bat.

He certainly *looked* real.

"Go ahead and get behind the plate," he said, gesturing at the wide, flat rock they'd placed at one end of the field to mark home base.

Brittany started heading for it.

"Hey, wait," Nathan called, and ran after her. He reached out and put his Yankee cap on her head. "There. You need that to keep the sun out of your eyes."

"Thanks," she said, grinning. The hat *did* help to reduce the glare, but that wasn't the only reason she liked wearing it. It made her feel special, sharing a hat with a boy. She wondered if Camisha and Lacey had ever done that. Probably not . . .

"Okay, now," Nathan called from the little hill he'd designated as the pitcher's mound. "Ready?"

"Ready," she said, taking her position, holding the bat poised.

"Good. Make like Reggie Jackson," he said.

He wound and pitched.

Make like Reggie Jackson, Brittany told herself as the ball sailed toward her.

Then it struck her.

First the thought.

Then the ball.

She gasped and jumped backward, dropping the bat and reaching up to rub her head as the ball plunked to the ground and rolled away.

"Hey, Brittany, are you all right?" Nathan asked, running toward her.

"Yeah, I'm . . . I'm fine," she managed to say.

He stopped a few yards away, and she stared at him.

Reggie Jackson had hit three home runs in the '78 World Series. That was what he had said.

That, and that he'd seen the game.

But if Nathan was seventeen years old now, how could he *remember* something that had happened back in 1978?

For a long moment, Brittany and Nathan stood there, looking at each other. And as they did, something happened to the sun.

In a matter of seconds, it vanished, and the sky became ominously dark.

Nathan looked up. "It looks like rain," he told Brittany. "We'd better run for it."

She just nodded, still staring at him. Her mind was whirling. She didn't know what to think, what to say, what to do . . .

"Run for it!" Nathan repeated, but this time more urgently, as earsplitting thunder disrupted the late afternoon silence.

She sprang into action as the sky opened up and rain started pouring down.

She started running, across the field, and then along the path, instinctively taking the hat off so she wouldn't lose it, and clutching it tightly against her as she went.

She ran and it felt wonderful—the cold rain stinging her face as thunder and lightning crashed around her. The storm was noisy and scary and powerful, and it drowned out her thoughts, drowned out everything but her pounding heart and her heavy breathing as she ran.

She didn't look back, didn't look to see if Nathan was with her, she only ran and ran and when she reached the fork in the path in front of the fountain she didn't hesitate, but turned toward home and kept running.

Finally, she was dashing up the front steps of the big wooden Butterfield house. On the porch, trembling and out of breath, she finally stopped.

Taking a deep breath and wiping the sweat and rain from her forehead, she looked behind her.

Nathan wasn't there.

She hadn't expected him to be.

But she was still clutching his Yankee cap.

So he had to be real.

But what about the '78 World Series?

*   *   *

"Close call, Nathan," Angela said as soon as he got back.

"I know." He ran his fingers through his damp hair. "I can't believe I slipped like that. Now she thinks I'm some kind of weirdo. I'm supposed to be helping her."

"Well, everyone makes mistakes."

"Even angels?"

"Of course. That is, until they earn their wings."

"At this rate, I'll never earn mine."

Angela didn't say anything to that.

Nathan reached up and patted his bare head. "She still has my Yankee cap."

"I know."

"Guess that's the least of my problems. What am I supposed to do next?"

"You'll figure it out," Angela told him.

"How?"

"Something will come to you."

Nathan closed his eyes and shook his head. "I can't believe I had to resort to a thunderstorm to bail myself out of that mess. That's so . . . amateur."

"Don't worry, Nathan," Angela said, patting his arm. "Come on. Let's go watch the Yankee game. It's just starting—a doubleheader. That'll make you feel better."

"Okay," he said glumly.

But first, he made a silent promise to Brittany.

Don't worry, kid—everything's going to be okay. For both of us.

Brittany sat in front of the television staring vacantly at *Jeopardy*, which was Barbie's favorite show. Her sister was next to her on the couch, answering questions out loud along with the contestants. She got nearly everything wrong, of course—but every so often, she hit on a correct response, and then she would jump up and shout, "*Yesss!*"

Brittany couldn't stop wondering about Nathan.

She'd decided that she must have heard him wrong—that he must not have said '78 World Series. Maybe it was '88, or something. Or maybe he was just kidding when he'd told her he'd watched it on television . . .

"*What* is China!" Barbie shouted at the TV set, then, a second later, said, "Wrong. Darn."

But Nathan hadn't acted like he was kidding. And he wasn't really the kidding-around type, from what Brittany could see. Not like her father. Mr. Butterfield prided himself on having a sense of humor. He was always telling people, "A man *has* to have a sense of humor when he's alone in a household with five women."

"*Who* is Abraham Lincoln!" Barbie called out,

bouncing excitedly on the cushion. "Wrong. Darn."

But then, there *was* something a little strange about Nathan. Well, maybe not *strange,* exactly. Just . . . different. He wasn't like anyone Brittany had ever met before. He was so—nice. Look at the way he'd returned her book bag. And the way he was teaching her how to hit a softball.

What was he getting out of it?

Nothing.

That was what was so odd.

And she had to wonder, again, why he bothered with her.

And when was she going to see him again? They didn't have plans to meet and she had no idea how to get in touch with him.

"*What* is a hot dog!" Barbie shouted at the television screen. Then she jumped up and screeched, "That's correct? *Yesss!* I'm a genius! Don't you think I'm a genius, Britt?"

"Yup," Brittany said absently, fingering the still-damp Yankee cap she held in her lap.

She *did* have Nathan's hat. So she'd *have* to see him again sooner or later, to give it back.

And maybe when she saw him, she'd ask him again about the World Series.

And about his last name.

And where he lived.

And why he was bothering to be her friend when no one else seemed to want to.

Chapter Seven

"Hey, Brittany, what are you doing Friday night?" was the first thing Camisha said when Brittany met her and Lacey on the corner Wednesday morning.

"Friday night? Nothing, why?"

"You are now." That came from Lacey, who was bobbing her red head excitedly as they fell into step together, heading toward school.

"I am?" Brittany looked from her back to Camisha, who was wearing a mysterious smile. "What am I doing?"

"You're going out on a triple date!" Camisha exclaimed.

At first, Brittany was too stunned to speak. Then she managed to say, in a small voice, "With a *boy*?"

"Of course, with a boy!" Lacey shook her

head, like she couldn't believe Brittany could be so dense.

Actually, Brittany suddenly *did* feel stupid. Why couldn't she seem to grasp what her friends were telling her?

A date . . .

A *date?*

With a boy . . .

With a *boy?*

What boy? And why would he want to go out with someone he didn't know? Why would *she* want to go out with someone she didn't know? Why would she want to go out on a date at all?

She didn't even know how to talk to a boy— except Nathan. But that was different.

"He's Quent's cousin," Camisha was saying, "and we're fixing him up with you because he's coming to stay with Quent's family this weekend—and because we think you guys would hit it off," she added hastily.

Brittany just looked at her.

"His name's Troy and he's from P-A," Lacey contributed.

"P-A?"

"Pennsylvania, Britt," Lacey said, again wearing that *I can't believe how thick she is* expression. "And Quent says he's cute."

"*Quent* says he's *cute?*" Somehow, Brittany couldn't picture Quent saying something like that. "*Cute?*" she repeated doubtfully.

"Well, Quent *described* him to us, and we think he sounds cute," Camisha clarified. "He has blond hair and he's tall."

"Oh."

"*Oh?*" Lacey echoed. "We fix you up with a cute boy from P-A and all you can say is *oh?* We thought you'd be really psyched about it, Brittany."

"I am," she lied. "It's just that I don't think my parents would want me to go out on a date yet."

"So don't tell them," Camisha said with exaggerated patience, like Brittany was a young child. "Do you think I told my parents about Jerry? They have no clue."

"Besides," Lacey said, "it's just to a party."

"What party? Where is it?"

Lacey shrugged. "Some ninth grader's house. Listen, Brittany, did your parents ever *tell* you that you're not allowed to date yet?"

Brittany thought about that.

Lacey had a point. It *hadn't* exactly come up— probably because Mr. and Mrs. Butterfield had never considered the possibility that someone would want to take Brittany out on a date. It wasn't like she was pretty and popular, or like any boy had ever paid attention to her before.

With the twins, dating *had* been an issue in middle school. They were always begging their parents to let them date, but they hadn't been allowed to until this past summer. Still, they had always been giggling on the phone with boys, or going to parties where there were boys . . .

Brittany had never talked to a boy on the phone. And she had never been to a coed party, either.

In fact, Nathan was the one and only boy she'd ever really talked to for any length of time. But that was different. Hanging around with Nathan wasn't a *date* . . . was it?

Had she been dating a high school boy without even realizing it?

"Well?" Lacey asked impatiently.

"No, I guess my parents never said I couldn't go on dates," Brittany told her.

"Then you're not really lying to them if you don't tell them," Camisha said in a *there, it's all settled* tone.

"I can't wait to tell Quent that it's all set!" Lacey said.

But I didn't say I'd go! Brittany wanted to point out.

Somehow, though, she couldn't say it. All she could seem to do was nod and smile and try to look and sound enthusiastic as Lacey and Camisha chattered about their big night out as they walked the rest of the way to school.

Because, as terrified as she was at the thought

of an actual date with an actual boy at an actual
ninth grade party, she was secretly thrilled that
her friends had decided to include her.

Maybe now things would get back to normal,
for real.

And maybe not.

Brittany was walking down the hall on her
way to gym on Thursday afternoon when someone bumped into her from behind. Hard. So
hard she almost fell.

She managed to regain her balance, then
turned around to see Joey Kulaga standing there
with two of his friends.

"Ooops!" he said loudly. "Sorry. It was an *accident.*"

Brittany's heart started beating like crazy.

"It's okay," she said in a tiny little voice, hoping she didn't seem as terrified as she felt.

She turned and started walking toward the
gym, looking straight ahead and trying not to
panic.

She'd taken a few steps when it happened
again.

"Ooops," Joey said behind her, and went flying into her back.

This time, Brittany was sent sprawling onto
the ground. Her book bag flew in one direction,
her glasses in another.

For a second, she was so stunned she could only stay there, on the floor, on her hands and knees. She heard Joey and his friends laughing, and then some of the other kids in the hall started in, too.

"Sorry," Joey said from somewhere above her. "It was another *accident*, I guess." She heard him laugh again, and then the sound faded as he walked on down the hall.

Brittany felt tears springing to her eyes.

No! Don't cry—whatever you do, don't cry, she warned herself. She focused blurrily on the tile floor, afraid that if she blinked or looked up, the tears would spill over.

That would be the ultimate humiliation—worse than anything Joey Kulaga could do to her.

Crying in middle school—she'd never live it down.

"Are you all right?" a voice said above her. A male voice.

For a second, she didn't respond. Then she took a deep breath and looked up.

Even without her glasses, she recognized him.

"Did you get hurt?" Dustin Plumb asked. And even without her glasses, she could even see the concern on his face.

"No, I'm fine," she lied, wiping quickly at her watery eyes and trying not to wince as she got stiffly to her feet. She glanced around the floor for her glasses and book bag.

"Here," Dustin said, holding them out. "I made sure I grabbed the glasses before someone could step on them."

"Thanks." She took them and put them on, then accepted her book bag and slung it over her shoulder.

There. That was better.

She looked at Dustin again. Now that she was wearing her glasses, his face was in sharp focus. It looked more angular than ever, and she noticed a sprinkling of pimples on his forehead.

"You okay?" he asked again.

"Yeah," she said, feeling shy.

She wanted to tell him how grateful she was that he'd helped her, instead of laughing at her like everyone else had done. But somehow, she couldn't.

"Good," he said.

Then he gave an awkward little wave, turned around and walked away.

Slowly, Brittany headed toward the girls' locker room, keeping an eye out to make sure Joey Kulaga wasn't lurking ahead, waiting to jump out at her.

He wasn't, but she knew she hadn't seen the last of him.

It wasn't until she had started changing into

her shorts that she realized her left knee was scraped and bleeding.

She put on her shorts and went out to the gym teacher's office. Miss Rigby sat at her desk, making notes on a clipboard.

"What is it, Butterfield?" she barked, looking up.

"I . . . um, I hurt my leg."

The teacher peered at it and frowned. She looked more annoyed than concerned. "How?"

The last thing Brittany wanted to do was tell her she'd fallen. Miss Rigby already thought she was a klutz.

But would she be any more sympathetic if Brittany told her the truth—that an eighth grade boy had pushed her down in the hallway? Somehow, Brittany doubted it.

She just looked at the floor and shrugged.

The teacher sighed. "Go to the nurse's office, Butterfield. And you'll have to stay there the rest of the period. We're going outside for softball, and I can't have you wandering around looking for us."

Brittany nodded and left the office.

At least one good thing had come out of this horrible Joey Kulaga mess.

She would get out of taking gym for a day.

Then she thought about Dustin Plumb.

Make that *two* good things.

* * *

"Brittany, I heard what happened in the hall today," was the first thing Lacey said after school.

"Yeah, everyone was talking about it last period," Camisha told her, as the three of them started down the front steps.

"Is it raining?" Brittany asked, holding out her hand, palm up. A few drops fell on it. "It is." She put up the hood on her jacket.

"Brittany, didn't you hear a word we said?" Lacey asked impatiently, pulling her own hood up over her long, reddish hair.

Camisha's jacket didn't have a hood, so she took it off and draped it over her head, then said, "Yeah, Britt, everyone's talking about how Joey Kulaga beat you up in the hall."

"He didn't beat me up," Brittany said, irritated.

"Well then what happened? Someone said you were all bloody and had to go down to the nurse's office."

"I wasn't *all* bloody. Just my knee." Which was stiff and painful now. She fought the urge to wince when she bent it as she walked.

"Look Brittany, what, exactly, happened?" Camisha demanded. "I mean, we're your best friends. The least you could do is tell us."

Brittany looked from her to Lacey. They both seemed to be waiting.

"Joey pushed me down. That's all," she said at last.

"That's *all?*" Lacey looked at Camisha.

"That's pretty bad, Brittany," Camisha said. "I mean, getting pushed down, in front of everyone, by an eighth grade boy is pretty bad."

Brittany shrugged. "Can we talk about something else?" she asked. "Please?"

There was a pause.

"Yeah, I guess," Lacey said. "Tomorrow's Friday. Are you excited about your date?"

"Uh-huh." Actually, Brittany was anything *but* excited. She dreaded it.

"Uh, listen, Britt, whatever you do, don't tell Troy what happened with Joey," Camisha said. "I mean, you don't want him to think—"

"I thought we weren't going to talk about Joey anymore," Brittany interrupted.

"Okay, okay, we're not. I just thought I'd tell you, in case you—"

"She won't tell him, Camisha," Lacey cut in. "I mean, Brittany's not *stupid*, you know?"

"Of course she's not stupid. I just wanted to, you know, give her some advice. Since she's not really used to talking to guys, or anything."

Suddenly, Brittany wanted more than anything to tell Camisha and Lacey about Nathan.

She wanted to say, "I am *so* used to talking to

guys, and not little baby eighth graders, either!"

But she couldn't bring herself to do it. Part of her didn't want to share Nathan with anyone.

And part of her was afraid her friends wouldn't believe her. She could just see them exchanging a glance and saying something like, "Yeah, sure."

And what proof did she have? She didn't know Nathan's last name, or where he lived, or even whether she'd ever see him again.

In fact, sometimes, she herself wondered if he was real. Maybe he *was* just a figment of her imagination. Then she remembered that she *did* have his baseball cap. But what would that prove to her friends? The cap could be anyone's.

She said nothing.

As they walked the rest of the way home through the gray drizzle, she kept quiet and thought about Nathan, wondering when—and if—she was going to see him again.

It wasn't until she'd said goodbye to Lacey and Camisha at the corner that she realized something.

They'd both thought Joey Kulaga had beaten her up, and yet neither of them had even bothered to ask if she was all right.

The only person who had done that was a total stranger, Dustin Plumb.

And Brittany knew exactly what Lacey and Camisha would think of *him*.

* * *

"You're awfully quiet tonight, Brittany," Mrs. Butterfield observed at the dinner table that night.

"I am?" Brittany asked blankly.

"You haven't said two words since we sat down," her father pointed out. "And since when do you pick at spaghetti? It's your favorite."

"Guess I'm not that hungry," Brittany told him shortly, and pushed her plate away. "Can I be excused?"

"Not yet," Mr. Butterfield said. "Whether you're hungry or not, this is family time. We're supposed to be enjoying this time together, talking and sharing what happened during the day."

Across the table, Brittany saw the twins roll their eyes at each other.

But Barbie promptly piped up, "I got a ninety on the Christopher Columbus test, Dad."

"Great!" Mr. Butterfield said. "How about you, Brittany?"

"I didn't take a Christopher Columbus test."

He grinned. "That's my girl—you have the Butterfield sense of humor. Come on, Brittany— tell us what you did in school today."

"Nothing much," she mumbled. "Just, you know, went to classes and stuff."

"Did you ever find out about joining the school newspaper?" Mrs. Butterfield asked, rolling some spaghetti onto her fork. "Remember how Mrs. Dolin encouraged you to pursue your writing in middle school?"

"Yeah, but . . . I don't think I'm going to."

"Why not? Brittany, you have a lot of talent. I'd hate to see it go to waste," her mother protested, then put the spaghetti into her mouth.

"What do I always say? Be a joiner, Brittany," her father advised heartily. "Keep active. Get involved."

Across the table, the twins looked at each other again.

"Yeah, but Dad, joining the *Keelan Khronicle* isn't exactly—well, you know . . ." Brooke said.

Brittany looked up at her.

So did Mr. and Mrs. Butterfield.

"Isn't exactly what?" asked Mrs. Butterfield.

"You know . . ." Brooke said, and turned to Beth for help. "It's not . . ."

"She means, none of the cool kids write for the newspaper," Beth said. "It's more like the— well, not the losers, exactly, more like the . . . I don't know, I guess, losers is kind of—"

"Beth," Mr. Butterfield said in a warning tone.

"*I* wrote for the school newspaper in junior high and high school," Mrs. Butterfield said cheerfully. "And I wasn't a 'loser.' Was I, Jack?"

"Nope," Mr. Butterfield said, popping a meatball into his mouth. "Your mother was one of the most popular girls in Keelan Grove. And the prettiest, too. And naturally, she married the most popular, handsomest guy in town, if I do say so myself."

He and Mrs. Butterfield beamed at each other.

Brittany squirmed in her seat. She hated when they acted this way, all sappy. Just as much as she hated when they tried to pry into her life.

"Anyway," Brooke said, shooting a disgusted glance at their mooning parents, "don't feel like you have to join the paper, Britt. There are tons of other things you can do."

"Yeah, like student council, and drama club..." Beth said.

"And cheering, and color guard . . ." Brooke added.

"And safety patrol," Barbie contributed. "I *love* being on the safety patrol. You get to wear a banner, and a badge, and every Friday you get to—"

Brittany couldn't take it anymore. She jumped up and glared around the table. "Why can't everyone just leave me alone?" she burst out.

There was silence. Her family stared at her, every one of them looking shocked.

"Brittany, what's wrong?" Mrs. Butterfield asked.

"We were only—" Beth started, but Brittany interrupted her.

"You were only being nosy and obnoxious," she accused, hating herself even as she said it, but somehow unable to stop. "You think you know everything. You all act like you know everything. Well, you don't! None of you knows *anything* about me!"

She shoved her chair back and stormed out of the dining room, clomping up the stairs to her room.

Just before she slammed the door shut behind her, she caught her father's amused voice saying, ". . . like this now, what's going to happen when she turns thirteen in a few months?"

Leave it to her family to write the whole thing off to adolescent angst.

Back when the twins were thirteen, her parents were always teasing them about being moody and unpredictable.

Didn't they know Brittany was different?

Didn't they understand that this was serious?

That her life was a total mess?

And that, no matter what she did, things kept getting worse?

Chapter Eight

On Friday morning on the way to school, Lacey and Camisha could talk about nothing but the triple date.

Brittany could think of nothing but how much she wanted to get out of it.

She wanted desperately to say, "Listen, you guys, I've changed my mind. I don't want to go after all."

But she knew exactly what would happen if she did that.

She could kiss her friendship with Lacey and Camisha goodbye.

And that was the last thing she wanted to do. She *needed* them—even if she didn't *like* them very much lately.

So when Camisha said, "Just think, Brittany, in less than twenty-four hours you'll be going on your first date," Brittany smiled and said,

"Yeah, I can hardly wait."And when Lacey asked, "Did you tell your parents you're sleeping over my house tonight?" Brittany smiled again and said, "Yup, they said it was fine."

Even though she hadn't told her parents about that yet. It wasn't that she hadn't intended to do it. But after the fiasco at the dinner table last night, she'd spent the rest of the evening in her room, trying to concentrate on homework.

She'd heard her father leaving for work, and she'd heard the *Jeopardy* theme music coming from the living room, and she'd heard the telephone ringing every twenty minutes or so, and the twins' pounding footsteps and shouts of "I'll get it!"

She had told herself she was glad everyone left her alone.

Even so, she kept expecting her mother or one of her sisters to come upstairs and knock on her door to make sure she was all right. And when no one did, she felt even worse than when they were all prying into her life.

"Do you think they were suspicious?" Camisha asked now. "I mean, do you think they believed you when you said you were sleeping at Lacey's?"

"Why wouldn't they?" Brittany asked. "And besides, we, uh—we *are* sleeping at Lacey's, aren't we?"

"Of course we are," Lacey said. "But my mom is going to a concert in Cleveland, remember? So she won't be back until way past midnight. I thought we already talked about all this, Britt. You know, how we get to stay out as late as we want? That's the whole point."

"Oh." Brittany tried to look enthusiastic. "That's right. I guess I just forgot."

She thought longingly of the old days, when she and Camisha would sleep over at Lacey's. The three of them would order pizza with everything on it and watch scary movies on cable and stay up until past midnight playing Truth or Dare or trying to have seances with Lacey's Ouija board. Had that really only been last year?

It seemed like ages ago.

Now here they were, sneaking out on dates with boys.

Oh, well, Brittany told herself, *maybe it'll turn out to be really fun.*

But somehow, she didn't think so.

School went by in a blur that day. Brittany spent every class worrying—about her date, about Joey Kulaga, about whether she'd ever see Nathan again.

As she sat in the auditorium alone at lunchtime, eating her soggy peanut butter sandwich, she couldn't help wishing he would show up

unexpectedly, even if it was just to get his baseball cap back. She'd been carrying it around in
her book bag, just in case she ran into him.

And in case she started doubting that he was
real. The hat, after all, was proof that he actually
existed—unless she was imagining the hat, too.
But every time she took it out of her bag and ran
her fingers over it, she was assured that it was
really there.

Touching the hat made her feel a little better
about everything in her life.

Actually seeing Nathan would make her feel
a *lot* better.

But he didn't come, and by the end of the day
she felt totally miserable inside. As she walked
home with Lacey and Camisha, she made sure
her glum mood didn't show on the outside.
Once again, she forced herself to go along when
they giggled and chattered excitedly about their
big date.

As soon as she got home, Brittany locked herself in the bathroom with a copy of her mother's
Style and Flair magazine and a quilted bag of
cosmetics she'd snuck out of the twins' bedroom. They would be furious if they caught her
borrowing their stuff, but they had cheering
practice and wouldn't be home for hours.

Brittany found an article on makeup—"Ten
Easy Tricks to Create a Sensational New You"—
and spent the next hour following it to the letter.

But it wasn't easy to put on eye makeup when you couldn't wear your glasses to help you see what you were doing. And how did people manage to hold their hand steady enough to put on liner and lipstick without getting it all over the place?

When Brittany was finished, she put her glasses back on, stepped back from the mirror, and looked.

Instead of a Sensational New You, she saw a total disaster.

Her face looked unnaturally orange—what was up with that liquid foundation she'd used? Her eyes were like black smudges, and her mouth was a red smear. And the bold slashes of pink blush that were supposed to define her cheekbones had instead turned her into a clown.

You can't go out looking like this, she told herself.

Besides, she felt so . . . icky. Like her face was so caked up with stuff that if she smiled, it would crack.

Not that she felt like smiling.

She took off her glasses, rolled up her sleeves, and started scrubbing. When she was finished, she looked normal again, though her face looked a little pinker than usual.

She tossed *Style and Flair* into the wastebasket without even glancing at the other article she'd planned to follow—"From Limp to Luxurious: How to Add Bounce and Shine to Dull Hair."

Forget it.

She was going to show up looking like herself, and if Quent's cousin didn't like her, that was too bad.

She picked up the makeup bag and was about to walk out of the bathroom when there was a knock on the door.

"Is someone in there?"

"Dad?"

"Yeah," he said, sounding groggy. "Brittany?"

"Yeah." She grabbed a towel from the linen closet and held it over her arm so that it concealed the bag, then opened the door. "Go ahead," she told her father, who stood there in the sweat pants and T-shirt he always slept in.

He yawned. "Thanks. How was school?" he asked as she brushed by him.

"It was great," she said brightly.

"Really?" He sounded surprised. "That's what I like to hear."

She started down the hall, then remembered something and turned around just as he was about to shut the bathroom door behind him. "Hey, Dad?"

"Yeah?"

"Can I sleep over Lacey's tonight?"

"I guess," he said, still sounding sleepy. "You haven't been to a slumber party in quite awhile, have you?"

"Uh, no, not really."

Slumber party.

It sounded so innocent.

She could just imagine what her father would say if he knew that she was really going to be going out to a ninth grade party with a strange boy from out of town.

But he didn't know.

He would never in his wildest dreams imagine that Brittany would do something like that.

All he said was, "Have fun—and call Mom in the morning if you need a ride home. It's supposed to rain."

The bathroom door closed behind him, and a moment later she heard the shower running.

Brittany sighed and tried to ignore a fierce stab of guilt.

She snuck the makeup bag back into her sisters' bedroom, then headed for her own room to change her clothes.

Have fun . . .

The words kept echoing in her ears.

Have fun . . .

Yeah, right.

*   *   *

"You're wearing *that?*" Lacey asked as soon as she opened the door and saw Brittany standing on the step in front of her mother's condo.

Brittany nodded and looked down at herself. She had on a pair of jeans and a sweater, which was exactly what Lacey and Camisha had said they were going to wear.

Except . . .

Except that Lacey had on tight black jeans that hugged her slim shape. They were tucked into suede boots that had at least a two inch heel. And her charcoal-colored sweater was snug-fitting and had a V neck.

Brittany saw Camisha standing behind her. She had on tight, faded blue jeans tucked into boots that were identical to Lacey's. And her navy sweater hugged her curves and was tucked into the slender waist of her jeans.

In contrast, Brittany looked lumpy and frumpy as ever. Her jeans were just *jeans*, baggy and still stiff and dark with newness. She'd bought them right before school started because her old ones had grown too tight over the summer.

And she was wearing a white turtleneck under an oversized pale pink cardigan sweater that was embroidered with little blue flowers around the neck and down the front. On her feet were her most comfortable white sneakers. She'd even taken the time to clean them with detergent and a paper towel before she'd left home.

But obviously, that wasn't going to cut it.

Brittany looked up at Lacey and Camisha and fought the urge to squirm.

"Listen, Britt," Camisha began, "it's not that you don't look just fine . . ."

"Because you do," Lacey jumped in. "It's just that you look kind of, um . . ."

"Casual," Camisha supplied. "You know, kind of casual for a date."

"But you guys said to wear jeans and a sweater . . ."

"I know we did," Lacey agreed, looking uncomfortable.

"Yeah, you're right, Brittany," Camisha said. "It'll be fine. Maybe if you just take off the turtleneck and—"

"Take off the turtleneck?" Brittany stared at her. "I can't do that. I'll look half-naked."

"She's right, Camisha," Lacey said. "Her cardigan would be open practically down to her belly button."

"It was just a thought." Camisha shrugged. "Why don't you come on into the bathroom and let me do your eyes, then?"

"Do my eyes?"

"You know, eyeliner, mascara, eye shadow . . ."

Brittany noticed that Camisha had apparently "done" her own eyes, and probably Lacey's, too. They were both wearing heavy makeup. Too heavy.

"Uh, no thanks," Brittany said. "I don't want my eyes done."

"Why not?" Lacey asked. "She did mine, see?"

"I see. I just don't want mine done. I'm allergic."

Camisha and Lacey exchanged a doubtful glance.

"Fine," Camisha said, throwing her hands up. "You can skip the makeup. But maybe Lacey can do your hair."

"Do what to my hair?" Brittany asked suspiciously.

"You know . . . fix it up a little," Lacey said. "Come on into my mom's bathroom. She has all kinds of gunk."

Brittany sighed and decided it was easier just to give in. "Fine," she told her friends. "Go ahead and gunk me."

Chapter Nine

A half hour later, Brittany found herself waiting on a dark street corner, her hair stiff and high over her forehead. She'd tried touching it after Lacey was finished, only to find that it no longer felt like hair at all. It felt like a cross between cotton candy and straw.

It *looked* like a cross between cotton candy and straw, in Brittany's opinion, though Camisha and Lacey had assured her she was glamorous and "sexy."

Sexy? Brittany had thought, looking in the mirror. She didn't think she looked sexy. She didn't even *want* to look sexy.

But here she was, supposedly sexy and about to meet her first date.

"Are you nervous?" Camisha asked, stamping her feet on the sidewalk as if she were freezing. Actually, she might be, considering how flimsy that sweater of hers was. But Brittany suspected it was more that she was jittery from nerves, even though she and Lacey kept trying to act casual about the whole thing.

"Nervous? Yeah," Brittany admitted.

"Don't be," Lacey advised. "It's no big deal."

"Yeah, it'll just be fun," Camisha said. "Just going to a party with a couple of guys—no big deal."

"Whatever." Brittany shrugged.

"Just think, maybe you and Troy will hit it off in a major way," Lacey told her.

"Maybe." Brittany imagined what that would be like. Maybe she and Troy would fall madly in love. What happened when you fell in love? She thought about movies she had seen.

She imagined dancing the tango with Troy— but that wouldn't work. She couldn't dance.

She imagined going for a long moonlit walk by the ocean—but that wouldn't work either. There was no moon tonight, and the only beach around was on Lake Erie, which was still too far away unless you drove, which Troy didn't—did he?

"How old is Troy, anyway?" she asked Lacey.

"I have no idea." Lacey wasn't looking her in the eye. "I guess he's, like, Quent's age. You know, thirteen . . . or maybe fourteen."

"*Fourteen?*" she repeated. What was she

doing going out with a maybe-fourteen-year-old boy?

What was she doing going out with *any* boy?

"You guys . . . ?" she said in a weak voice. "I think I—"

"Shhh! There they are!" Lacey said, jabbing her in the side.

It was too late to back out now.

There was nothing to do but go through with it.

Brittany gulped and stared at the three shadowy figures that were walking toward them.

As they drew closer, she was vaguely aware of Camisha and Lacey giggling and whispering excitedly to each other.

She recognized Quent, in his football jacket.

And Jerry, in his football jacket.

And now that they were under a streetlight, she could see the third boy.

Troy.

Her date.

He was tall—at least six feet. And broad-shouldered. And blond.

And really good-looking—so good-looking, Brittany thought Brooke and Beth would be impressed.

He was wearing tight, faded Levi's jeans and a jean jacket.

He was smoking a cigarette.

And, Brittany realized as he stopped a few

feet away, he looked more like a man than like a boy. How old *was* he?

"Hi, Quent," Lacey said in the giggly, high-pitched voice Brittany had heard her use at the mall that day. "Hi, Jerry."

"Hey, guys," Camisha said.

"What's up?" Jerry asked.

Quent just looked at Brittany, and then at Lacey, who suddenly seemed nervous.

"Uh, Quent, you remember Brittany Butterfield, right?" Lacey didn't wait for an answer. She turned to his cousin. "And you must be Troy, right?"

The stranger nodded and took a drag on his cigarette.

"Well, this is Brittany," Lacey said.

Troy's gaze flicked over her, then over Camisha, and came to rest on Brittany. Feeling her face grow hot, she shifted her weight to her other foot and tried to find her voice.

Finally, she managed a squeaky, "Hi."

He muttered something that *could* have been a greeting, but she wasn't sure.

She couldn't mistake the look he sent Quent and Jerry, though. It said, *You guys are dead.*

Obviously, Troy-the-man wasn't pleased to be matched up with Brittany-the-seventh-grade-loser.

"Well," Camisha said brightly, "let's go!" She fell into step next to Jerry and they headed down the street toward the party, which was a few blocks away.

Quent immediately grabbed Lacey and pulled her off to the side. They seemed to be having a whispered argument, and a few times, Quent looked over at Brittany.

Then Lacey stood on her tiptoes and whispered something in his ear. Her hand was resting on his arm.

Brittany saw him smile.

Then Lacey asked him something else.

Quent shrugged and Brittany heard him say, "Sixteen, I think."

Instantly, she knew what they were talking about.

Brittany snuck a peek at Troy. He was shuffling along beside her, still smoking his cigarette.

He looked kind of—moody. Maybe even angry.

And who could blame him?

He was sixteen and gorgeous, and here he was, out on a blind date with a pudgy, nearsighted, braces-wearing twelve-year-old.

Brittany thought about Nathan.

He was even older than this Troy guy. But he never acted this way around her. He talked to her like she was a regular person.

She felt a lump rising in her throat.

Nathan, where are you? she wondered.

She would give anything to be with him right now, instead of with this sulky stranger from P-A.

In fact, she would give anything to be anywhere else, anywhere at all—even in gym class with Miss Rigby yelling at her.

For a moment, she was struck with the wild thought that if she just closed her eyes and wished really hard, she could somehow zap herself out of this situation.

And she actually tried it, after casting a sideways glance at Troy to make sure he wasn't looking at her as they walked along.

Of course he wasn't. He was looking straight ahead, his mouth set in a grim line now that he'd finished his cigarette.

Brittany squeezed her eyes closed, concentrated, and counted to three.

Then she opened them again.

She was still walking down a dark street with a stranger.

She should have known better.

Get a grip, Brittany, she told herself, disgusted. *There's no such thing as magic, and you know it.*

The party wasn't like a party at all.

At least, not like any party Brittany had ever been to.

She didn't know what she'd been expecting—

certainly not Pin-the-Tail-on-the-Donkey or crepe paper and balloons. But she'd vaguely imagined something more—well, partylike. Maybe a long refreshment table, maybe someone's mother taking coats at the door.

Instead, the house was overrun with kids and noise. Music blasted, there were no familiar faces, and all the lights seemed to be turned off.

Brittany tried to stick close to Camisha and Lacey as they made their way inside. Troy, who still hadn't said two words to her, vanished as soon as they walked through the door.

"Want to go to the bathroom?" Lacey shouted at Brittany when they'd reached the kitchen with Quent and Jerry leading the way.

"Yeah," she said, relieved at the thought of escaping, even if it was just for a few minutes.

Lacey and Camisha led the way up a back staircase. The second floor of the house was dark, too, but there were fewer people up here, and it was quieter.

They found a bathroom and all three of them went in. Lacey closed and locked the door behind them.

"Well?" she asked Brittany. "What do you think?"

"Of what?"

"Of *Troy!*" Camisha said. "Isn't he cute? I knew he sounded cute."

"He's definitely cute," Brittany said. "But you guys, he's *sixteen*. And he hates me."

"He doesn't hate you," Lacey told her, standing in front of the mirror and smoothing her hair.

"Then why is he ignoring me?"

"Maybe he's just shy," Camisha suggested.

Brittany shook her head. "No way. I think I should leave."

"Leave?" Lacey took her eyes off her reflection and turned around. "You can't leave!"

"Why not?"

"Because you're on a *date*," Camisha told her.

"But I don't even know where Troy is!"

"But I promised Quent—" Lacey started, then stopped and turned quickly back to the mirror.

"You promised him what?" Brittany asked.

"You know," Lacey said.

"What?"

"She promised him that, uh, you know," Camisha said, "that she'd get him a date for his cousin."

Suddenly, Brittany understood. Lacey and Camisha hadn't done this for *her*. They had done this for themselves.

And that wasn't all. They hadn't even told Quent that she, Brittany, was the girl they were going to fix up with his cousin. That was why he'd looked so surprised to see her, and why he'd pulled Lacey aside to argue.

Brittany's friends had probably figured that if Quent knew in advance who Troy's mystery date was going to be, he'd say *no way*.

Brittany stared at Lacey, who couldn't even meet her gaze. Then she stared at Camisha, who shifted her eyes to the floor, looking guilty.

And she suddenly wondered why she'd thought she needed them.

"When it comes to friendship, you guys really stink," she said impulsively, and realized it was the first honest thing she'd told them in weeks.

They both looked up at her, startled.

"Brittany—" Camisha began, then stopped.

"Yeah?" Brittany asked, narrowing her eyes.

"Nothing," Camisha mumbled. "Forget it."

"Come on, Brittany, don't act this way," Lacey said. "We're your friends, and you're treating us like dirt. We went through a lot of trouble to get you a date."

"You did not, Lacey. You only got me this date because Quent asked you to find someone for his cousin, and you obviously didn't have anyone else to ask."

"That's not true," Lacey said, but Brittany could tell by the look on her face that it was.

"Oh, come on, Lacey. You know that you guys haven't wanted anything to do with me lately. You think you're too cool to hang out with someone like me. All you care about is yourselves. And boys. And parties that aren't even like parties. And makeup, which by the way looks *really* stupid on both of you."

With that, Brittany turned away from them and walked out the bathroom door. Just before she slammed it shut behind her, she looked back over her shoulder and caught a glimpse of the shocked, insulted expressions on both Lacey's and Camisha's faces.

That should have left her feeling satisfied.

But all she felt, as she walked down the unfamiliar hall in the unfamiliar house, was hollow inside, and more alone than ever.

Chapter Ten

If Brittany had been paying attention to what was going on around her, she might have noticed that she was being followed when she first left the party.

But she was lost in thought as she shoved her way back through the crowd of strangers, finally making it to the door. The cool air outside felt good, and so did the silence of the deserted street.

It didn't occur to her to be afraid . . .

Not until she had walked about a block and heard the footsteps behind her.

Startled, she spun around just in time to see someone diving into the bushes along the sidewalk a few yards back.

Her heart started pounding wildly. She turned and started walking again, more quickly this time. She had to fight the urge to run. If she did, whoever was behind her would know she'd seen them.

She scanned the street ahead. There were a few houses that were set way back from the sidewalk, and some businesses—a dry cleaner's and a hair salon—that were closed for the night.

Her own house was blocks away, and to get there she had to walk past the park, which would be shadowy and deserted at this hour. It would be the perfect place for whoever was following her to catch up to her, drag her into the trees, and attack her.

Despite her growing panic, Brittany kept walking briskly, looking straight ahead.

What else could she do?

She couldn't turn around and go back to the party. Whoever was lurking behind her would catch her for sure.

She couldn't go to one of the houses on the street and ask for help. Some were lit up, but that didn't mean anyone was home. And if she stayed close to the street, maybe a police car would drive by and she could flag it down. Maybe someone, *anyone*, would drive by.

At the corner, Brittany paused and cast a quick glance over her shoulder. Sure enough, she saw someone dive into the bushes again. This time, he was slow enough for her to see that it was a boy. A large boy.

Joey Kulaga.

Brittany had known it was him all along. He must have been at the party and seen her leave.

Swallowing hard, she turned left.

As she rounded the corner, a dark figure jumped out in front of her and grabbed her arms.

Brittany opened her mouth to scream, but she was so shocked and terrified that nothing came out. All she could do was make a weak, gasping sound.

"Shhh . . . it's me," someone whispered.

"Nathan?" Shocked, she stared up at him.

"Come on," he said, and pulled her into the shadows. She looked around and saw that they were in an alley between two low brick buildings.

"What are you doing here?" she asked him in a low voice.

"What are *you* doing here, all by yourself, at night?" was his response. "This part of town isn't all that safe, Brittany."

"I know, but—"

"And besides, Joey Kulaga is following you."

"You *know* who Joey Kulaga is?" she asked in disbelief.

"Yeah, I know who he is," Nathan said in a tone that told Brittany exactly what he thought of Joey. "Shhhh—he's coming. Stay there. I mean it, Brittany, don't move."

She nodded numbly, wanting to warn Nathan not to mess with Joey, but he was already moving away from her. He crept forward and peeked around the front of the building.

Brittany saw a shadow pass by.

Then Nathan slipped out and disappeared onto the sidewalk.

A few seconds later, she heard a bone-chilling scream, and it hadn't come from Nathan.

"No! Please, don't hurt me!" someone pleaded.

Could that have been *Joey?*

"Please, let me go," the voice said again.

It *was* Joey.

Brittany couldn't imagine a bully like him being afraid of Nathan, of all people.

Then she heard another voice. "Leave Brittany Butterfield alone," it said.

It didn't belong to Nathan—at least, Brittany didn't think it did. It was too low, too eerie . . .

"I will," Joey said shakily. "I swear. I'll leave her alone."

"If you don't, I'll get you," warned the voice. "Now get out of here."

Brittany heard pounding footsteps that quickly faded down the street. A moment later, Nathan stood on the sidewalk, beckoning her to come out of the alley.

He was grinning.

"Nathan? What happened?" Brittany asked, staring at him.

"I just scared Joey away."

"That was you? It didn't sound like you."

Nathan shrugged. "I disguised my voice. Come on, I'll walk you home. I don't think he'll be bugging you ever again."

"I hope not," Brittany said doubtfully. Somehow, she couldn't imagine Nathan scaring Joey away, even though she'd heard the whole thing. And how had Nathan made his voice that scary?

They started walking toward her house, and now the night didn't seem anywhere near as threatening. It was actually kind of peaceful, strolling along through the shadows with Nathan.

"You know, I have your Yankee cap," Brittany told him.

"I know."

"I'll give it back to you when we get to my house."

"Thanks. I've had it for, uh, a long time," Nathan told her.

"I would have given it to you sooner, but I didn't know where to find you."

"It's okay."

She was about to get up her nerve and ask him where he lived, what his last name was, all of it, when he said, "You know, Brittany, everything's going to be okay."

Caught off guard, she looked at him in surprise. "What do you mean?"

"I know you're miserable at school these days, but it won't always be this way. You won't always feel like you don't fit in."

"How did you know that's how I feel?"

He shrugged. "I just know. And I promise you that things are going to get better. You'll see."

"Well, if Joey leaves me alone, it will help," Brittany said. "But I don't have any friends at all now. Lacey and Camisha are history. And everyone still thinks I'm a klutz, and a loser."

"That'll change."

"That's what you think."

"That's what I *know*," Nathan told her firmly.

To humor him, Brittany nodded. "Okay, sure. Maybe you're right," she said.

But in her heart, she knew he wasn't. She was never going to fit in. She was always going to be a friendless loser.

Too quickly, they were standing on the walk leading up to her house. Brittany looked at the windows and saw that the light in her parents' room was on. That meant her mother was in there, probably reading in bed.

"I'll go in and get your cap," she told Nathan. "Wait right here."

He nodded and sat on the bottom step as she walked quietly up onto the porch.

She fished her key out of her pocket, let herself into the house, and made her way as silently as possible up the stairs. In her room, she grabbed the familiar baseball cap, then crept back down the stairs.

She hesitated just inside the big, old-fashioned front door and looked out through the glass at Nathan sitting on the step. The sight of him was so reassuring, after all she had been through, that for a moment she had to fight a lump that rose in her throat.

He was a stranger, really, and yet he'd been so good to her. He'd actually cared.

Maybe he was right.

Maybe there *was* hope for her.

Brittany opened the door and stepped out onto the porch, pulling it closed behind her.

She started across the porch, forgetting to be careful. Her foot landed squarely on a loose board that responded with a loud *creak*.

Uh-oh.

Sure enough, a moment later, the porch light flicked on.

"Is someone there?" her mother's voice called from inside.

"It's me, Mom," Brittany said.

She glanced down at Nathan, who had stood and was looking up at her. "Here, catch," she said to him, and hurriedly tossed the Yankee cap in his direction.

He caught it. "Thanks, Brittany."

"You're welcome." She waved and turned around just as her mother opened the door and stuck her head out.

"Brittany? What are you doing out here? I thought you were sleeping over at Lacey's." Mrs. Butterfield was wearing a long flannel nightgown and had her finger stuck between the pages of a book.

"I was. But we, uh, had a fight, and I, uh, walked home." How was she going to explain Nathan?

"Alone?" Her mother sounded horrified.

Alone? Brittany frowned and looked over her shoulder at the sidewalk in front of the house.

It was empty.

How had Nathan managed to disappear so quickly?

"Yeah, alone," Brittany said, puzzled but relieved as she turned back to her mother. "It was no big deal."

"Brittany, how many times do I have to tell you that if you need a ride, you should call home?" Mrs. Butterfield held the door open for her. "Come on inside. You never know what kind of creeps are lurking out there after dark."

Brittany thought of Joey Kulaga. *You can say that again,* she told her mother mentally, stepping into the warm foyer.

But there were good guys out there, too.

"What are you smiling about?" her mother asked, looking closely at her after shutting and locking the front door again.

"Am I smiling?" Brittany asked.

"Yes, and it's about time. I haven't seen you smile in weeks."

"I guess I haven't felt like it in weeks," Brittany admitted.

"Want to talk about it? I could make us some hot chocolate," Mrs. Butterfield offered.

"Not especially," Brittany told her, then saw her mother's disappointment and added quickly, "But you can still make us some hot chocolate."

"Yeah?" Mrs. Butterfield looked pleased.

"Sure," Brittany said, suddenly feeling warm and cozy inside.

"Okay, come on." Laying a hand on Brittany's shoulder, Mrs. Butterfield led the way to the kitchen. "Maybe you'll at least tell me what on earth you did to your hair!"

"Well?" Nathan asked Angela, putting his Yankee cap back on his head and patting it contentedly. "What did you think?"

"Nicely done," she told him. "I especially liked what you did to that bully."

"Joey?" Nathan shrugged. "I was a sight he won't soon forget. Do you think I went a little overboard?"

"The green face and tentacles were a bit much, but I guess he had it coming."

"You bet he did, after how he treated Brittany."

"You really came through for her."

"She came through for herself first, though," he pointed out. "Telling those two so-called friends off like she did. It's about time."

"You can say that again."

Nathan smiled and peeked in on Brittany again. There she was, sitting at the kitchen table with her mother, drinking hot chocolate and laughing about something.

"She's really going to be all right, Angela," he said contentedly. "See? All she needed was a friend. That's what I said all along. There's only one thing I'm worried about."

"What's that?"

"What's she going to think when I don't come back?"

Angela shrugged. "Don't worry. Eventually, she'll forget all about you. That's how it's always been. It's easier that way."

"I guess," Nathan said, feeling a little wistful. "But I wish she knew that I'll still be watching over her."

Angela patted him on the shoulder. "Some day, she'll know, Nathan. Some day, you'll meet her again. Just like I met you."

He smiled at her, then down at Brittany.

Chapter Eleven

Monday morning, Brittany walked to school alone. She hadn't expected Lacey and Camisha to be waiting on the corner for her, and when they weren't there, she wasn't disappointed.

Actually, it was a relief to stop working at a dying friendship. Anything was better than pretending to be someone you weren't—even being alone.

Then again, she wasn't alone. Not really.

She had Nathan. He cared about her. He was her friend . . . a *real* friend. The next time she saw him, she'd thank him for everything. Maybe she'd even invite him to come over for dinner some night . . .

Daydreaming about Nathan was a pleasant way to fill the blocks between her house and school.

When she got there, she made her way up to her locker as she did every day.

At the top of the stairs, she caught sight of a familiar face in the crowded corridor.

Before she knew what she was doing, she found herself opening her mouth and calling out, "Dustin! Hey, Dustin!"

He stopped and looked around. He didn't seem to see her, and started walking again.

Brittany pushed past a group of girls who were gossiping in front of a water fountain, and caught up to him. "Dustin?" she asked, touching his sleeve.

He turned and saw her. And the moment he did, he broke into a smile. "Hi," he said.

"Hi. I'm Brittany Butterfield—"

"I know."

"You do?"

He nodded. "You introduced yourself to me one time."

"Yeah, but I didn't think you'd remember." She felt a warm little glow. "Anyway, I just wanted to tell you—I mean, ask you, if you still need writers for the school paper?"

"Definitely. Are you interested?"

"Definitely." She grinned at him.

"There's a meeting in room 106 after school tomorrow. Can you make it?"

"Sure."

"Great."

For a second, they just stood there smiling at each other. Then Brittany said, "Well, I guess I'd better go. Thanks a lot, Dustin."

"Thank *you*," he said, and waved at her.

Feeling pleased with herself, Brittany headed to her locker.

It wasn't until English class that she heard about Joey Kulaga.

Kara and Jade came rushing over to her desk as soon as she sat down.

"Brittany!" Kara said, like they were old friends. "How's it going?"

"Fine . . ."

"Did you hear about Joey?" Jade asked.

"What about him?"

"He was attacked by an alien on Friday night!"

Brittany stared at Kara. "He was *what?*"

"Attacked by an alien," she repeated. "And the alien told him to stay away from *you!*"

Brittany burst out laughing. "Is that what he's telling people? An alien?"

"Yeah," Jade said, her eyes serious. "He said it was a huge creature, green all over, with tentacles. And fangs."

"Wow," Brittany said blandly.

"And he said it threatened him," Kara said.

"He's so scared of you that he's not even in school today."

"He's scared of *me?*" Brittany couldn't believe it. Joey Kulaga, scared of her.

Joey Kulaga, so scared he'd made up some crazy story about an alien attacking him.

Brittany couldn't wait to tell Nathan.

She decided not to wait until she happened to bump into him again. She'd track him down herself.

"Can I help you?" the gray-haired secretary in the office of Keelan Grove High asked Brittany curiously.

"Um, yes," she said, walking briskly toward the woman's desk and trying to sound professional. "I need to find one of your students."

"Well, school has already let out for the day," the woman told her.

"I know that. I just need to find out his last name."

"You do, hmmm?" The woman looked amused. "Are you a detective?"

Yeah, right. She's making fun of me. Brittany frowned. "No. And this is serious."

"I'm sure it is, sweetie. Who is it that you're looking for?"

"His name is Nathan."

"Nathan." The woman pushed her chair back and stood up.

For a moment, Brittany expected her to go call the principal and tell him that a middle school student had barged into the office.

Instead, though, the woman crossed to a computer terminal and sat down in front of it. She looked up at Brittany expectantly. "What grade is he in?"

Relieved, Brittany said, "I'm not sure. I think he's a senior. He's seventeen."

"Hmmm. Let me see . . ." The woman began typing on the keyboard, then settled back and looked at Brittany. "The computer is searching for everyone named Nathan in the senior class."

"Thank you."

"You're welcome." The woman still looked amused, but at least she was helping.

A moment later, she said, "Here we go. The only senior named Nathan is Nathan Timberson."

Nathan Timberson.

He was the one Beth had mentioned. The short, stocky, blond Nathan.

"Wrong one," Brittany told the secretary. "Are there any Nathans in the junior class?"

"Just a moment." The woman pressed more keys, then shook her head. "No Nathans."

Brittany frowned. "How about sophomores?" She doubted that a seventeen-year-old would be a sophomore, but then again, you never knew.

The woman pressed more keys, and a moment later, shook her head. "No other Nathans in this school."

"But that's impossible. Maybe you missed one."

"Sweetie, this is a *computer*. It doesn't make mistakes. If there was another Nathan in Keelan Grove High, it would have come up with him."

Brittany just stared at her.

Nathan had lied about going to school here.

How could he?

Why *would* he?

Did he even exist?

Nothing made sense.

Shaking her head slowly, Brittany turned and walked out of the office.

"Sweetie?" the woman called behind her.

She turned around briefly. "Oh, yeah," she said halfheartedly. "Thanks."

Then she headed down the large, empty hallway and out onto the street. The school grounds were deserted.

Brittany walked slowly home alone.

The next day in gym class, Miss Rigby led them out onto the softball field, as usual.

And Brittany was the last one chosen for a team, as usual.

And when she stepped up to bat, her teammates groaned and whispered and giggled, as usual.

She ignored them.

She stood on the plate and gripped the bat, concentrating.

The pitcher wound up, released the ball, and it came sailing toward her in a blur of white.

This one's for you, Nathan, Brittany thought.

Then she swung.

The bat connected with something.

The ball!

It had actually connected with the ball!

Amazed, Brittany tossed the bat down and started running toward first base.

It wasn't until she felt it beneath her feet that she stopped, turned, and saw the center fielder retrieving the ball and shouting "I've got it!"

"Nice hit, Butterfield," Miss Rigby called, and Brittany heard her teammates clapping behind her.

Elated, she looked up at the sky.

Thanks again, Nathan . . . wherever you are. Whoever you are. Thanks for everything.

"You're welcome," Nathan told Brittany softly, reaching up and taking off his Yankee cap. Just for a moment, he clutched it against his chest. Then he carefully settled it on his head again, just as Angela showed up.

"Nathan!" she said excitedly. "I have news!"

It took him a second to focus. "News? What news?"

"It's about you. And it's good."

"How good?"

"The best." She grinned at him. "You've earned your wings! You made it, Nathan. To heaven!"

"I made it!" he repeated, then threw his arms around Angela. "I made it! To heaven!"

"You sure did. Come on, let's go. Everyone's waiting."

He stepped back. "Everyone? Who's everyone?"

"Well, your grandfather, for one—"

"Grandpa Oakley? I never knew him. He died when I was a baby."

"He's been waiting a long time to meet you."

Nathan smiled fondly, then asked, "Who else is there, Angela?"

"Oh, just—everyone," she said again.

"Do you mean . . ." He paused to take a deep breath, then let it out. "Do you mean that Babe Ruth is there?"

Angela nodded. "It took him awhile, but yup, he's in heaven."

"And Lou Gehrig?"

Angela nodded again.

"And Thurman Munson?"

Another nod.

Nathan broke into a grin. "I've died and gone to heaven."

"Exactly," Angela said with a giggle. "Now come on."

"Just a second," Nathan told her, hearing the distant crack of a bat on a ball.

He snuck another peek at Brittany.

She was just leaving third base and heading home as her teammates shrieked her name excitedly.

"Go for it, Brittany," Nathan said softly.

And she did.

Nathan watched her until she'd crossed over home plate and a huge smile had settled on her face.

Then, smiling just as broadly, he straightened his Yankee cap, and turned back to Angela. "Okay, I'm ready. Heaven, here I come!"

Keep an eye out for *Henry Hopkins and the Horrible Halloween Happening*—coming soon!

Henry Hopkins and the Horrible Halloween Happening

Twelve-year-old Henry Hopkins is miserable. It's embarrassing enough that his mother is an artist, and not at all like his friends' mothers, who wear business suits and have high-powered corporate jobs. *Now* she just told him she's getting married on Halloween . . . to Shep, a guy who wears an earring and plays in a rock band! Henry decides that the only solution is to go and live with his *real* father. The only problem is, he's never met his father and doesn't know how to find him.

Then Henry meets a cool seventeen-year-old guy named Bryan. Bryan promises to help Henry uncover the truth about his dad. But strangely enough, as Halloween draws near, Henry starts getting to know—and like—Shep a lot better. Then, just before the wedding, Henry's mother tells him the truth about his father. Stunned and confused, Henry knows that Bryan is the only one who can set things straight. But suddenly, Bryan is nowhere to be found. . . .